THE EMPEROR'S DETECTIVE

THE EMPEROR'S DETECTIVE

PERCY ANDREÆ

WILDSIDE PRESS

INTRODUCTION

Percy Andreæ (1858–1924) was an English-American brewer and influential anti-prohibitionist during the early part of the 20th century. He was born in Clapham, London to a German father, Carl Andreæ of Frankfurt, and an English mother, Emilie Sillem. During the 1890s, Andreæ published short stories and novels, many of which first appeared in *The Windsor Magazine*.

His fiction drew on his roots, incorporating international mystery and suspense with adventure, set in the height of the Victorian era. The hero of "The Emperor's Detective" series is a British man-for-hire who finds himself working for a very interesting employer, one who has no qualms about assigning him impossible cases.

Andreæ immigrated to the United States in 1896. He settled in Cincinnati before moving to Chicago, becoming a U.S. citizen in 1914. Shortly after his immigration, Andreæ abandoned fiction writing for a career in brewing. He soon became involved in politics when the rising temperance movement threatened his livelihood. After the Anti-Saloon League made sweeping victories in the 1908 Ohio state elections, Andreae formed a resistance group, The National Association of Commerce and Labor, which fought temperance organizations on the national level. (It largely employed former state Senators and Representatives to further its work.) Andreæ died in Winnetka, Illinois, aged 65.

But back to our interests, his books include:

Stanhope of Chester: A Mystery (1894)
The Mask and the Man: A Novel (1894)
The Signora: A Tale (1895)
The Vanished Emperor (1896)
A Life at Stake (1902)

Here, I am pleased to present the complete 6-part series "The Emperor's Detective" which ran serially in *The Windsor Magazine* in 1898. The texts have been edited, punctuation modernized, and revised where necessary for clarity.

Enjoy!

—John Betancourt
Cabin John, Maryland

THE INCIDENT OF THE SEVERED FOREFINGER AND THE HOUSE IN THE WALDSTRASSE

I am a gentleman adventurer. I make this statement frankly and unequivocally, so that no misunderstanding on the subject may arise hereafter. There is, in my opinion, no earthly reason to be ashamed of the title. To be reduced to the necessity of living by one's wits is no disgrace, provided one is possessed of the requisite wits to live by. As for myself, they have so far never failed me, and I am afford to snap my fingers at certain stiff-necked noodles of my acquaintance who, while careful on occasion to treat me with due outward respect—for I enjoy no mean reputation as a marksman—do to my certain knowledge shun my society as if it were not fit for reputable men.

I do not give a fig for the opinion of such fools. A couple of hundred years ago qualities such as mine would have conducted a man to fame, fortune, and honour. Living as I do in this humdrum nineteenth century, two or three hundred years behind my time, I am forced to rest content with the consciousness of my deserts, and to seek adventure for the mere pleasure it brings, not for the honour it yields.

This by way of preamble to a series of adventures which in any time save the present would have placed me beyond the need of earning the precarious livelihood upon which I now depend.

It was about two years from the date of present writing that I landed in Berolingen with a couple of hundred pounds in my purse, a troublesome scar on my leg—the relic of a bullet wound received during the siege of Plevna—and in my pocket one or two introductory cards to officers in the Arminian capital, bequeathed to me by a late comrade-in-arms in colonial East Africa. I had taken service about ten years before in the Turkish Army, since when and the time I speak of I had borne arms under more flags than I care to enumerate. There is always trouble somewhere on the globe, and, though I have at times found it difficult to make both ends meet, I have never suffered from lack of employment. My last resting-place had been

Wittichau, a comparatively small garrison town in Silesia, where I had come within an ace of entering into the bonds of holy matrimony and settling down for the rest of my days to a staid and sober family life. From this fate I was mercifully preserved by the fickleness of the object of my affections, a young woman of exceptional attractions, who, after flirting with me for three weeks in the most outrageous manner, suddenly disappeared from her home with an obscure adventurer who, as I subsequently learned, had all along been paying her clandestine attentions.

I mention these latter facts as they have no little bearing upon the adventures I am about to relate, the first of which occurred within a fortnight of my advent to the Arminian capital. I had spent the greater part of those two weeks in hunting up the men to whom I had introductions, and ascertaining from them what prospects I possessed of obtaining military employment in Arminia. The result had been somewhat disheartening, for I found, in the first place, that my good friend from East Africa had considerably overrated the esteem in which he was held by the officers to whom he had commended me; and, in the second place, that, in spite of the fact of my having held honourable commissions in several European armies, my entry into the service of his Majesty the Emperor Willibald of Arminia was barred by seemingly insuperable difficulties. Accustomed as I was to a life of activity, time soon began to hang heavily upon my hands, and, disgusted at the cold reception afforded me by those upon whose assistance I had so surely reckoned, I was already determining to quit Arminia altogether, and direct my steps at haphazard into some other quarter of the world, when an event occurred which altered, for a period at least, my whole fortunes, and in its sequel brought me within a hair's breadth of realising my most cherished dream.

Occupied with the thought now uppermost in my mind, the devising of some new plan for my future, I was sauntering late one night along the border of the beautiful Thiergarten which adorns the western portion of the city, when I chanced, on turning a corner where the forest takes a sharp bend towards the east, upon a scene of a somewhat startling character. Beneath a huge beech tree, with his back set against the trunk, stood a man with a drawn sword, defending himself against the joint attack of three stalwart fellows. The latter, as it seemed to me, were not armed, or at least, if they were, they made no use of their weapons. Their object apparently was to secure their man, whether for the purpose of robbery, or with some other intent, I could not say. A glance sufficed, however, to show me that, in spite of his valiant stand and the advantage he possessed in being armed, the man at the tree could not long resist the onset of such overpowering odds. Hastening to the spot, therefore, I seized the sturdiest of his three assailants by the neck, and using him as a kind of battering ram against the other two, created a sudden diversion that gave the attacked party a moment's breathing space.

The result, so far as I was concerned, proved rather different from what I had expected, for, upon recovering from their surprise, the trio, as of one accord, turned about and directed their attack against me. In the twinkling of an eye the fellow I had seized wrenched himself free, and, casting his arms round my neck, endeavoured to throw me to the ground. Had I had only him to deal with I should have laughed at his efforts. But my attention was necessarily divided between him and his two comrades, one of whom, as I now saw, had an ugly-looking knife in his hand, with which he danced around me as I struggled with my assailant, evidently awaiting his opportunity to give me a home thrust.

It was the deuce of a predicament, and I inwardly cursed myself for my folly in meddling in a business that didn't concern me. Engaged as I was in dodging one man's knife, whilst another was using his utmost efforts to throttle me, I had no leisure to bestow any attention upon the man whose rescue I had foolishly undertaken. My breath was getting scant, and lights of various colours were beginning to dance before my eyes, between which I saw at intervals the silvery gleam of the stiletto upraised over my head. Suddenly it descended with lightning quickness, a sharp cry of pain, accompanied by a furious oath, followed, and I fell heavily to the ground. The grip upon my throat was released, but I must have lost consciousness for a few instants, for when I looked up the three villains were gone, and I was alone with the man to whose assistance I had sprung.

He stood gazing down upon my prostrate form with a cool, critical smile. In his right hand he held the short thin weapon I bad seen him using against his assailants, and in his left a kind of wooden scabbard, into which he presently returned the blade. The whole arrangement, as I now saw, was what is commonly known as a sword-stick.

"Holy thunder!" I exclaimed, raising myself and involuntarily speaking in English; "that was a narrow squeak."

My companion nodded.

"I am indebted to you," he said, speaking in the same tongue. "You are an Englishman, I see."

"At your service," I replied, "and a fool at that."

"Your name?" he asked.

"Walter Raleigh," I answered. "And yours?"

"A name to be proud of," he remarked, ignoring my question. "I trust it is borne by one who is not unworthy of his greater namesake."

He spoke English with so perfect an accent that I was in doubt whether he could he a native of Arminia, and, curious to learn whom I had so opportunely befriended, I repeated my query as to his name. But he once more coolly evaded an answer.

"We will see," he said. "We shall have time enough to become better acquainted. For the present it would be well for us to think of shifting our quarters here."

He bent down as he spoke, and, picking up an object which lay in the snow, regarded it for an instant with a grim smile. It was a human forefinger, cut off at the lower joint as clean as if severed by a surgeon's knife.

"By Jove, that's a dainty bit of work," I exclaimed, as he quietly wrapped the limb in his handkerchief and placed it in his pocket. The coolness of the whole proceeding tickled me greatly.

"Better a scoundrel's finger than your life, friend Sir Walter," he said. "I owed you a debt, and I have repaid it. We are quits."

"Rather far from quits," I cried, a good deal moved by this explanation of my escape from certain death. "The odds are yours, and you may count upon Walter Raleigh to make them even should occasion offer."

"We can discuss that later," he replied, regarding me sharply for a moment, as if weighing my words. "If you care to render me a service, maybe you will find it not entirely to your disadvantage to do so."

Without awaiting my reply, he emerged from the trees under which we had been conversing, and hailing an empty droschky that happened to pass sleepily along the boulevard, motioned me to enter it with him. I complied almost mechanically. He gave the driver his directions, and in another moment we were being whirled at a rapid pace towards the great Brandenburg Gate at the top of the famous Avenue of Limes.

The drive occupied but a few minutes, my companion's abode being one of the few smaller detached residences, surrounded by a garden, which are still left in that portion of the city. The vehicle had scarcely stopped at the front gate, when the door of the house was opened, letting out a flood of light into the dark night, and a man-servant came hurrying down the walk with a lantern in his hand to receive us. Having handed the driver a piece of money, he preceded us with his lantern and escorted us in this fashion into the house.

To say that the appearance of the interior, which was profusely illuminated, surprised me would be to understate the case. The effect was simply dazzling, and reminded me very forcibly, in everything except its size, which was small, of those brilliant fairy palaces we read so much of in tales of Eastern origin. It seemed almost as if the place had been fashioned after some such oriental model. Every room was furnished and appointed after a different artistic design. The costliest materials draped the walls and carpeted the floors, and ornaments of massive gold and silver, priceless vases, gems and cu-rios, met the eye wherever it turned.

Immediately upon my entrance, at a sign from my companion, I was taken in charge by the servant who had carried the lantern, and conducted to a large bath-room on the ground floor arranged in Moorish fashion, with a large pool in the middle and stone divans covered with silk cushions along the walls. A black attendant, with turbaned head and attired in long, loose robes girded round the waist, stepped forward to receive me, and after assisting me to disrobe, re-tired to a seat at the head of the bath, whilst I plunged into the tepid water and refreshed my limbs after the somewhat severe tussle in which they had been engaged.

Having taken my tub under these to me very novel circumstances, I was once more assisted into my clothes by my black friend, where-upon the servant who had brought me reappeared and conducted me to another room, where I found a table laid out with every possible delicacy. I had scarcely had time to look around me when my host himself entered by a door at the lower end. Taking his seat at the head of the table, whilst two servants placed themselves behind his chair, he motioned to me to join him, which I did without demur, proceeding to attack the good things set before me without waiting to be invited. The repast was excellent, the wines superb, and my spirits rising with the occasion, I was not backward in replying to the many questions regarding my birth, experiences, and general antecedents, with which my host plied me pretty freely during the course of the meal.

On one subject, however, I noticed that he maintained a curious reticence, cutting me short in a very peremptory manner when I questioned him upon it. It was the reason of the attack that had been made upon him that night. All I could gather was that he knew nothing of his assailants, nor of the object of their assault. Yet, from the general tenor of his conversation I felt sure that he had had some definite purpose in bringing me to his house, and I naturally connected it in my own mind with his adventure that night.

I was not left long in doubt on the subject, for, when the meal was over and the servants had retired at a sign from their master, the latter addressed me, without further preamble, as follows:

"From what you have been good enough to tell me, I gather that you are here in search of employment congenial to a character such as yours. Are you willing to accept such employment at my hands?"

"Provided it is compatible with the dignity and honour of a gentleman, certainly," I replied promptly.

"The service I should require of you demands two things—firstly courage, and secondly discretion. From what I have seen of you, I believe you to possess courage. Whether you have discretion is a question I am still left to solve."

I bowed. "And the service?" I asked.

"It is this. A few days hence a certain person will present himself under cover of night at a certain house in the north-western part of the city, where he will receive a packet of papers. Your task will be to secure this packet of papers and deliver it to me."

I rose. "This smacks of highway robbery," I said coldly. "I am ready to fight, but not to steal."

"The distinction docs you credit," he replied, without moving from his seat. "I may understand, then, that you refuse to render me this service."

"Unless you can prove to me satisfactorily that you possess some just claim to the papers you desire to secure by such unusual means, undoubtedly. You forget," I added, "that, although I am under an admitted debt of gratitude to you, I have as yet not even the honour of knowing your name."

"That is a defect easily remedied," he rejoined. "On the one condition, however, that you pledge me your word of honour never to mention the fact of your acquaintance with me to living soul. Are you prepared to do this?"

"Why not?" I answered with a laugh. "I have no confidential friends here, and my circle of acquaintance is but slight; you have my word."

"Good," he said simply. "My name is Heinrich von Retzow." He fixed his eyes keenly upon me as he spoke. "It is, perhaps, one that is not entirely unknown to you."

I gave a start of surprise. The name, as I need scarcely tell the well-informed reader, was none other than that of the famous, much-feared political detective who was currently believed to hold in his hand the fate of half the notables at the Emperor Willibald's court.

Certainly, I thought to myself, as I glanced round the sumptuously furnished apartment in which we were sitting and remembered the luxury of which every corner of the house gave striking testimony, the business of this man, if not exactly reputable in the strictest sense of the term, must be an unusually remunerative one.

"Will it content you," my companion went on, "if I assure you that the papers I desire to secure contain a state secret of vital importance to his Majesty the Emperor, into whose hands they will be delivered?"

"Why, that sounds somewhat better," I said, after a moment's reflection, "though I must confess I do not relish the task."

"I can promise you that it shall be followed by one which is perhaps more congenial to your taste," he answered. "I mean the tracking down of the gentleman who, but for my timely intervention, would undoubtedly have placed you beyond the need of the employment you are seeking. I have some personal curiosity to learn more of this personage."

"A difficult job," I remarked, "since I unfortunately never caught a glimpse of the fellow's face. Even if I came across him, I am afraid I shouldn't know him from Adam."

"You forget," he rejoined, "that he has had a mark placed upon him that will be difficult to conceal. We have a clue there which should make it easy to hunt down our man."

He pointed as he spoke to the mantelpiece, where I now saw for the first time, among the costly bric-a-brac ornaments that adorned it, a small bottle filled with a whitish fluid and containing a ghastly-looking object, which I recognised at once as the forefinger he had picked up from the snow.

I am not of a squeamish disposition, but I could scarcely repress a slight shudder of disgust at the sight of it.

"But let us return to our subject," my companion continued, as if we had been discussing the most ordinary topic in the world. "I have asked this particular service of you as a repayment of the debt you owe me. Of course, if you fear the danger it involves——"

"I fear no danger," I interrupted him, growing warm at the insinuation, "save dishonour. If I fail in this undertaking, who will guarantee me immunity from punishment at the hands of the law?"

"Ah, if you count upon failure," he said, turning away with a gesture of contempt, "let us break off at once. I sec I have misgauged you."

Whether it was design or not, he had touched me very cleverly at my weakest spot, and I exclaimed angrily—

"By heavens! no one shall say I am a coward. I am your man, then, let happen what may."

He resumed his scat quietly, and in a few terse sentences set forth the plan I was to follow, giving me the exact locality of the house I was to watch and the probable time of the delivery of the packet I was to secure. Having done which, he dropped the subject and fell into an easy discourse upon other matters, chiefly military, his object evidently being to set me talking about my adventures in foreign parts and the events I had participated in, for which he seemed to evince a curious interest. At last, the hour having advanced far into the morning, he rose abruptly and dismissed me without further ceremony, with an air of easy command that nettled me somewhat, though it became him marvellously well.

On thinking over the details of my adventure the following day, I had to admit to myself that I had acted very foolishly in undertaking the perilous mission imposed upon me. It is true I was fond of adventure, and the mystery attaching to the enterprise before me rather enhanced than lessened its charm in my eyes. But certain reports that had reached me concerning the doings of Herr von Retzow, whose reputation for scrupulousness was not of the best, rendered me a trifle uneasy as to the ultimate consequences to myself of the step I had undertaken. What if this man merely intended to use me as a tool to compass his own ends, and then to cast me aside, or perhaps make me his scapegoat in the event of his plan failing?

It was too late to retreat now, however, for my word was pledged, and I have never broken my word in my life.

Three days after the incident in the Thiergarten, I received a note, warning me to be on my guard that night. It was signed, "H. v. R.," contained an enclosure, and concluded with the following words— "Keep the enclosed, but use it only in the direst extremity."

The enclosure referred to was merely a visiting card, across which was written slantwise in hold characters—"Commending the bearer, Mr. Walter Raleigh, to the good offices of Colonel Heinrich von Stauffenberg."

The thing puzzled me, for there was no signature attached to it, unless a kind of flourish at the bottom, which looked as if the writer had been about to affix his name and had stopped short in the act, could be taken for a sign manual.

I placed the card in my breast pocket, however, and when night fell proceeded with the best heart I could summon upon my mission.

It was about eight o clock when I arrived at my destination, a house not dissimilar in size and general exterior appearance to that which I had visited three days before. The garden, which fronted it on the Waldstrasse, and through which a drive led to the main entrance at the side (front doors are not unfrequently side doors in Berolingen), was fairly deep and thickly grown with shrubs, affording excellent hiding-places for persons on errands such as mine. Nor was I slow to avail myself of the shelter it offered. The neighbourhood was quiet and almost deserted, the night being cold and very dark, and it was an easy matter for me to vault over, the fence that separated the garden from the street and ensconce myself unobserved among the bushes on the lawn.

I was prepared for a vigil of possibly an hour or two, yet, as one quarter after another struck upon the neighbouring church clock without any one appearing, I began to grow impatient and suspicious that I had been sent there on a fool's errand. Once I fancied that I heard a stealthy footstep pass by me upon the gravel drive and approach the house. The signal by which I was to recognise my man was a sharp double rap with a cane against the house-door. But I listened for the sound in vain, and concluded that I had been the victim of my own imagination.

I grew the more convinced of my error when I presently heard the further gate swing and the unmistakable crunch of a man's footsteps upon the gravel path. There was evidently no attempt at concealment here. The man, whose figure I could perfectly well distinguish through the bushes behind which I was hidden, passed rapidly up the drive, hesitated an instant when he reached the house, and then disappeared down the side walk leading to the entrance. The next moment I heard a sharp double rap upon the door, and I knew the moment for action had come.

The suspense was short. Apparently the delivery of the packet, being a preconcerted event, required no exchange of civilities between the parties concerned, for, within two minutes of the double rap at the door, the man reappeared once more in front of the house. Having meanwhile shifted my position in such wise as to be able to spring out and confront the fellow at the corner, I was just parting the undergrowth in front of me in order to dart out unhindered, when something quite unforeseen occurred which altered my plans entirely.

I had been forestalled by someone else. Instead of one solitary figure on the pathway I now saw two, and they were engaged in a desperate struggle. The glimmer of steel in the dim light shed by a lamp near by showed me that one of the two was armed, but I could not distinguish which. I heard the words—"The packet, you scoundrel, or I'll run you through the body"; then a violent scuffle, as the combatants shifted their ground on the gravel, a desperate oath or two, and, before I could make up my mind whether to step out and intervene or not, the couple had separated, and my man was speeding down the driveway as fast as his legs would carry him.

I let him run unhindered, for I saw at a glance that his assailant had possessed himself of the packet. He stood regarding it for an instant with evident satisfaction, then turned sharply on his heel, and, instead of following the other out of the place, made straight for the house door. Although I followed him as swiftly as I could without betraying my presence, I was only in time to see him open the door with a key and disappear into the house, slamming the door behind him.

My consternation at this unexpected turn of things was complete. Here was a dilemma indeed. Did this man belong to the house? And dared I beard him in his own dwelling and take the papers from him by force? The notion savoured too much of downright burglary to be pleasant. Moreover, the man was armed with a sword, and though I carried a revolver—for safety sake—I scarcely reckoned on having to use it under such circumstances as these.

I was standing thus irresolute when of a sudden the loud, hysterical cry of a woman burst upon my ear. It came from the house, and simultaneously two shadows appeared on the blind of one of the windows of the lower floor. From the gestures made by the two figures it was evident that the one, a female, was pleading for something; whilst the other, a man, was holding her at arm's length. The shadows vanished again almost immediately, but I could hear the voice of the woman continue to implore and threaten alternately, then break off for a while into hysterical sobs, and presently resume its pleading tones once more.

In itself there was nothing particularly startling about all this. But there was something distinctly startling to me in the fact that I knew the voice of the woman. Strange as it may seem, it was none other than that of the girl who had jilted me six months before in the Silesian garrison town, and had eloped with another.

In an instant my resolve was taken. The window, on the blind of which the two shadows had appeared some moments ago, gave on to a low verandah easily accessible from where I stood, and, what was more important still, it was, as I now observed, slightly open. Without waiting to consider the full consequences of what I was doing, I swung myself on to the verandah, pushed open the window, and sprang into the room.

The effect of my appearance was somewhat dramatic. The woman, who proved indeed to be no other than my faithless love from Silesia, fell back on the sofa with a loud shriek; whilst the man, who was attired in the undress uniform of an Imperial guardsman, sprang forward, sword in hand, as if to attack me. Possibly something in my posture caused him to reflect, for, instead of using his weapon, he stopped short and asked—

"What do you seek here?"

I pointed to the packet he was holding in his hand, which had evidently been the subject of the conversation I had interrupted.

"I would trouble you for those papers," I answered, thinking it best to brazen out the situation.

"You scoundrel!" he ejaculated, "you shall pay for this insolence!"

He raised his sword as he spoke, and advanced threateningly towards me. But I was now on my mettle.

"You had better let us settle the matter amicably," I said, drawing my revolver, "or I shall be compelled to use arguments that I would prefer to avoid."

I covered him with my revolver as I said these words, and he drew back aghast.

"What!" he exclaimed. "You dare to threaten my life?"

"Precisely," I answered. "I shall shoot you where you stand within fifteen seconds, unless you deliver me those papers. I have authority for my action, and it will be at your peril that you challenge it."

People who have had the kind of experience in life that I have had will be aware that a determined attitude often masters the most desperate situations. The present proved to be a wise in point. There was just one moment's suspense, then a flash as of sudden intelligence in the man's face, and the next instant the packet of papers flew at my feet.

I did not stir. No doubt he guessed the reason, for he turned deliberately on his heel and left the room.

"We shall meet again," he said, as he closed the door behind him.

"I shall be charmed," I answered, with a mock bow, and picked up the packet.

A minute afterwards I heard the house door slam very violently, and knew that my man had left the house.

I now turned my attention to the woman. She had risen from the sofa, and stood looking at me with eyes of terror.

"Mr. Raleigh?" she whispered.

I bowed.

"I am honoured," I said ironically.

"By what right do you claim that packet?" she asked.

"By the same right as he who was robbed of it ten minutes ago in that garden," I said, answering at random.

"Is that true?" she asked, her eyes lighting up strangely; and then, as I merely shrugged my shoulders, she added, "Are you one of Herr von Retzow's men?"

I opened my eyes in surprise, for this was a staggerer. But I did not hesitate a moment.

"At your service," I said.

She still looked doubtful.

"Mr. Raleigh," she said again, and her voice had that touchingly pleading sound that I knew only too well, "will you pledge me your word of honour as a gentleman and a soldier that you intend to deliver that packet into Herr von Retzow's hands?"

This time I could answer with a good conscience in the affirmative.

"Unless the gentleman who just handed it to me should meanwhile succeed in regaining possession of it, most assuredly," I replied.

She drew a breath of relief.

"You had better hasten away," she said. "If you give him time he will find means to thwart you yet."

"Is he your husband?" I asked.

She nodded.

"And you fear him?" I said.

Perhaps there was a touch of anger in my question, which she noticed, for once more that strange light came into her eyes, and she looked at me with a searching gaze.

"You are not deceiving me, Mr. Raleigh?" she faltered. "If you knew all, you would pity me and help me."

"By God!" I exclaimed, much moved by her sadly subdued manner, which was so different from that of the proud, wayward girl I had known six months ago; "if he has injured but one hair of your head I will make him rue it."

"Give me the packet," she said, with sudden energy.

I hesitated.

"I am but a weak woman," she went on scornfully, noticing my reluctance. "Are you afraid I would keep it?"

I placed the packet in her hands. She tore the cover open with nervous fingers, extracted a paper, and handed it to me.

"Read that," she said.

I glanced at it. It was a certificate of marriage between one Ernest Frederick, Count of Lausitz, and Anna Theodora, daughter of district inspector of customs, Ludwig Volkmar, of Wittichau, in Silesia.

My lip curled.

"A count," I said. "So I have the honour of addressing Madam the Countess?"

She appeared not to notice the sarcasm.

"Do you know," she asked, "who it is that bears the title of Count of Lausitz?"

"I am afraid that my genealogical knowledge does not extend so far," I remarked. "I have never heard of a Count of Lausitz."

"Possibly not," she said. "It is one of the titles borne by the Duke of Friedrichsburg."

"The Duke of Friedrichsburg?" I exclaimed, at first scarcely comprehending her full meaning. "Do you refer to the Emperor's brother-in-law?"

"I mean the Emperor Willibald's brother-in-law," she answered.

"But," I stammered incredulously, "is not this man your husband?"

"Unless that paper lies, certainly," she replied somewhat proudly. "It is the only proof I possess of my marriage, for the leaf of the register on which it was recorded has recently been torn out and destroyed, by whose order I leave you to conjecture."

I stood dumbfounded. The whole thing sounded like a romantic fable. The Duke of Friedrichsburg, the unruly and somewhat notorious brother of the Arminian Empress was, I understood, on the eve of becoming betrothed to the beautiful young Princess of Bieberstein. Yet, if what I had just heard was true, he was already a married man, and the simple daughter of the customs inspector of Wittichau was, according to all law, moral if not actual, Duchess of Friedrichsburg and sister-in-law to the Arminian Empress.

"Are you sure," I asked, handing her back the paper, which she returned into the cover, "that this Herr von Retzow will prove the true friend you think him? This is a valuable paper you are parting with, doubly valuable, indeed, in view of the destruction of the original from which it is copied."

"Do you suppose me a fool?" she said irritably. "That paper in Herr von Retzow's hands will avenge me for my sufferings, and avenged I will be, though it should cost me my life and my honour," she added, looking like a handsome little fury.

"And you shall have my help, too, for the matter of that," I exclaimed, remembering with some bitterness that the man she now hated had been the destroyer of my pretty dream of six months ago.

"Against him?" she asked, an eager sparkle in her eyes.

"Why not?" I said. "You appear to forget that I, too, have an account to settle with this gentleman."

Upon my word, I believe she remembered nothing at all of my own courtship and the cruel treatment I had received at her hands, for she looked at me blankly for a moment and then merely said, in an absent way—

"You are right. I forgot. If I should require a friend, then, I will not fail to send for you. But now go quickly," she continued, with more animation. "You have delayed too long already, and every minute is precious."

Indeed, there was nothing more left for me to say or do, and, fearing that further delay might be dangerous, I placed the packet, which she now pressed upon me, in my pocket and took my leave.

I deemed it safest to make my exit by the same way that I had entered, and, having gained the street, walked swiftly in the direction of the main thoroughfare, where I knew I could obtain a conveyance to take me westward. I had not proceeded above fifty yards, however, before I observed that I was being shadowed. The fact in itself caused me no alarm, and I did not even think it worth while troubling to ascertain who my pursuer was. It was not detection I feared, for against that I could easily defend myself, but an attack, which might undo all I had so far achieved and cause my mission to fail on the very eve of success.

Merely hastening my footsteps, therefore, and keeping well in the middle of the road, to obviate any possibility of a sudden assault, I sped on towards the more frequented quarter where my safety lay. In the distance I could distinguish the figures of two policemen who were apparently engaged in a quiet chat at a street corner, and I felt that when I had once reached and passed them I should be well out of my danger, for the main street was but a couple of turnings farther on.

I was within a few yards of these men when a shrill whistle just behind me caused me to start and turn my head. As in a flash I recognised in the person following me the man whom I had forced to yield up the packet of letters. The next instant I was struggling in the grip of four strong arms which had seized me from behind, and I knew that I had been trapped. I fought desperately for a few seconds, and, had the contest been a fair and square affair, I believe now that I should have gained the day. But these devils would take no chances, and, before I could bring such skill as I possessed into play, I received a blow on the head from behind with a sharp instrument, and fell heavily to the ground.

I have but a faint and hazy recollection of what then occurred, for my senses came and went for a time intermittently and then left me entirely. Two scenes only have remained pretty clearly engraven on my memory. The first was a big, bare room very sparely lighted, with benches along the walls, and a desk-table, surrounded by a wooden railing, near the window. A police officer sat at this desk, and five or six others stood around, whilst I lay on a kind of stretcher upon the bare floor. I saw a strip of paper pass from hand to hand, and by the hushed voices of those who inspected it, and the almost scared expression upon the faces of every one present, I gathered dimly that it contained something of a character startling to my captors. Every now and then their eyes would turn, first in my direction with a look of anxious concern, and then towards the door, where presently a gentleman in civilian dress entered. The latter approached me, and lifting my head, inserted his forefinger, as it seemed to me, into the middle of my brain, whereupon the whole scene vanished strangely and made room for another.

This was a small, but comfortable and extremely clean chamber, where I lay with bandaged head upon a snow white bed. Here all was quiet and peaceful. Tender hands ministered to my wants and soothed my aching brow with some cooling fluid. Nothing could have been more delightful, had it only lasted. But this scene and the former one kept alternating and mingling and merging into each other, for how long I cannot say. All I know is that I woke up one dreary afternoon to find myself an inmate of the city hospital, where I lay, well cared for, though friendless, for about a fortnight, leaving at the end of that time with a pretty deep scar on the back of my head and a puzzled feeling as to how I had got there. The hospital authorities could tell me nothing, save that I had been brought there by the police and entered in the books of the hospital as a first-class patient. When I asked for my bill, however, I was merely told that it had been paid, though by whom and in what manner I tried in vain to elicit.

Needless to say, the packet which had been the cause of all my misfortunes was no longer in my possession. One of the first things I found, however, on rummaging the pockets of my clothes, was the card given me by Herr von Retzow. It had been a good deal crumpled and fingered, and upon mature reflection I came to the conclusion that its discovery upon my person by the police was probably answerable for the humane treatment I had received after my capture.

My first step, after my return to my lodgings, was to visit the house I had watched on that fatal night three weeks ago. I found it closed and deserted, but for a female caretaker who opened the door in answer to my repeated knocking, and informed me, upon my enquiry whether the Countess of Lausitz would receive me, that no Countess of Lausitz lived there, nor had any one of that name ever occupied the house to her knowledge. The last occupant had been a lady with some outlandish name, such as Ralli, or Rowley, or the like, and had left the place in a hurry three weeks ago for reasons best known to herself. For the rest, if I were curious, I was at liberty to apply to the police, whose interest in the house and its former tenant was deeper than she, the caretaker, found pleasant.

All this information, given in a tone of deeply injured dignity, fairly took my breath away, and I returned citywards a good deal downcast. Sitting in a well-known café on the Avenue of Limes an hour or two later, I was glancing through one of the back numbers of an English daily, when a paragraph under "Latest Intelligence" caught my eye. It ran thus—

"The sudden banishment from the Imperial court of Duke Ernest Frederick, the Empress's brother, has caused a considerable flutter in society circles here. The cause of his Highness's exile appears the more mysterious in view of the almost simultaneous arrival in the capital of the Dowager Duchess of Bieberstein, whose beautiful young daughter, the Princess Alexandrine, is generally reported to be the destined bride of the banished Duke. As this match, though strenuously opposed in certain illustrious quarters both on this and the other side of the channel, is known to be a pet scheme of his Majesty the Emperor, who believes in matrimony as the best means of checking the much talked of vagaries of his obstreperous relative, the unexpected transfer of the latter to an obscure provincial garrison at the very moment of the young Princess's advent to the Arminian court has naturally set all heads here a-wagging."

So the Duke of Friedrichsburg was exiled from court. Had Herr von Retzow had a hand in this? And if so, by what means? Scarcely by reason of the success of my mission, I thought.

I went back to my lonely lodging with a feeling of considerable despondency, due partly, no doubt, to my somewhat weak condition, but partly also to the sense of my failure, which nettled me deeply. The day had been an eventful one for me, but the chief event was still to come, for I had scarcely reached my rooms when my landlady placed a somewhat bulky and official-looking letter in my hands, which I hastened to open.

It contained two enclosures. One a short note without any signature, and couched in the following terms—"You have failed, my dear Sir Walter, but you have failed well. Let the enclosed be some compensation to you for what you have suffered. I shall expect to see you tomorrow before midnight."

I had scarcely cast an eager glance at the communication referred to, when I dropped it in sheer amazement at what it contained. This was nothing less than a formal document appointing Mr. Walter Raleigh, of Warden Court. Sussex—the seat of my family—to the post of Oberstallmeister—*Anglicé*, Master of the Horse—to her Serene Highness the Dowager Duchess of Bieberstein. It was signed, "Baron Rudolph von Brinkwitz, Master of the Ducal Household," and was accompanied by a short note from that dignitary informing me that, upon the strong recommendation of Colonel Heinrich von Stauffenberg, her Highness had been pleased to make the said appointment, and requesting me to be good enough to call at the Chamberlain's office early the next morning.

I hardly knew whether to regard the whole thing in the light of a hoax or not. There were two things, however, which, upon fuller consideration, left me no doubt as to the genuineness of the affair. First, the evident knowledge of my family possessed by Herr von Retzow or his friend von Stauffenberg, and, secondly, the nature of the office to which I had been appointed. I was considered the black sheep of my flock, it is true; but the flock I came from was of the oldest and purest blood in England. I am not accustomed to boast of my family connections, nor had I breathed a word of all this to Herr von Retzow, so that he must have been at some pains to ascertain my actual birth and rearing. As for the appointment itself, it was one for which anyone who knew me intimately would admit that I was peculiarly well fitted. There was a time, indeed, though I say it myself, when my fame as a daring horseman was on the lips of every man and woman who ever rode with the hounds in the south of England. To suppose, therefore, that Herr von Retzow—or von Stauffenberg—I began to fancy they were one and the same—had recommended me without a knowledge of these facts was out of the question. Yet whence had he derived his information? And what ends was he pursuing in thus promoting me?

I confess that these and other considerations, which I need not dwell upon, rendered me a trifle uneasy. Still, my pride was considerably tickled by the prospect before me, and I never for one instant entertained the notion of refusing such brilliant preferment.

It was indeed a strange and, as it seemed to me, almost unaccountable ending to my adventure with the packet of letters. But still more strange and unaccountable things were to happen in the sequel, of which I shall have to relate hereafter.

THE INCIDENT OF THE RUNAWAY HORSE AND THE FACE AT THE WINDOW

I was Master of the Horse to her Serene Highness the Dowager Duchess of Bieberstein. I chuckled to myself when I thought of what certain friends of mine would say if they could see me in my new exalted position.

Let no man think, however, that it was a sinecure. Far from it. The office, even in smaller principalities than that of Bieberstein, is to some extent one of honour, much coveted by the blue-blooded gallants who existatcourts; but it is also connected with a good deal of downright hard work. In my case I soon found that the chief service expected of me was that of teaching the young Princess what is known in Arminia as English riding.

I shall never forget the impression produced upon me by my first interview with my illustrious young pupil, whose loveliness, so often commented upon of late by the newspapers, was really no myth. The old Dowager Duchess, who had honoured me with a two minutes' audience upon my entry into the ducal household in Berolingen, was a stiff and starchy body, who, after eyeing me for fully ten seconds through a *lorgnon* with an immense handle, asked me if I spoke French, and, upon my replying in the negative, turned her back upon me and conversed for the remaining 110 seconds in that particular lingo with Baron von Brinkwitz, who had presented me. The Princess Alexandrine was of a different make altogether. She addressed me at once in English, extended me her hand, not to kiss, but to shake, and kept me busy for quite a quarter of an hour answering questions innumerable about London society folks, the latest English sporting news, and other similarly entertaining matters. She spoke our language with a slight accent, but remarkably fluently, interspersing her sentences with the sweetest little slang phrases that ever fell from the lips of a pretty girl. Altogether, she was an up-to-date young lady of the most approved type, full of spirit, and dash, and pluck, and so simple and unaffected in manner that you quite forgot, when she talked with you, that you were conversing with the daughter of a sovereign house, who was about to ally herself with the near relative of the most powerful army chief in Europe.

For there appeared to be little doubt that the chances of Duke Ernest with this sweet young princess were, in spite of his banishment, very favourable. The Duke was by no means ill-favoured. He had an engaging manner, and his reputation as a fast liver served, perhaps, rather to enhance than to lessen his charm in the eyes of an innocent girl, to whom wickedness, being an unknown and mysterious quantity, is correspondingly fascinating. Yet, pure and innocent as she was, it was the opinion of those who knew the Princess Alexandrine that, if anyone were capable of taming the rakish Duke, it was she, and it was not long before I coincided with this view.

I had not been installed in my new office more than a couple of days before I discovered that my surroundings were not all of a friendly character. I was looked upon with a good deal of envy by my fellow-servitors, and with unconcealed suspicion by those above me in rank and station. Among the latter, to my chagrin, I had to reckon her Majesty the Dowager Empress Fritz, to whom my young mistress, in her goodness of heart, took the first occasion to present me, thinking, no doubt, that, as an Englishman, I should be received with particular graciousness. Unfortunately, the reverse was the case. Her Majesty gave me, on the occasion in question, such indubitable signs of her disfavour that I turned red and white from sheer dismay, and the young Princess looked not a little embarrassed and displeased.

I attributed all this to the fact that I was believed to have been introduced into the Bieberstein household as a kind of spy in the employ of the Duke of Friedrichsburg's party, a circumstance, by the way, that annoyed and disturbed me a good deal; for, though I had learned that the mysterious Colonel von Stauffenberg, through whom I had received my appointment, was no less a personage than the military secretary of the Emperor Willibald, I had no reason to suppose that he was in any way interested in my humble person. My dealings were with Herr von Retzow alone, and to all appearances the service this gentleman expected of me was merely that of tracking and identifying the persons who attacked him that eventful night when I first formed his acquaintance.

Still, I harboured for some time secret hopes that the disfavour with which I was evidently regarded by the party of the Dowager Empress might one day be counterbalanced by the favour of one still more powerful than she. Truth to say, I had originally come to Berolingen with some hazy notion that I might possibly succeed in entering the personal service of the Arminian sovereign, for whose adventurous spirit I entertained a deep admiration. Herr von Retzow, to whom I had confessed these aspirations, had somewhat artfully hinted at the possibility of their fulfilment as a kind of general recompense for the faithful performance of such duties as he imposed upon me.

However, if I dwelt fondly upon such dreams, they were soon destined to be rudely dispelled, as the incident I shall now relate will show.

It occurred on one of Princess Alexandrine's morning rides in the Thiergarten, which it was my duty to superintend in person in my capacity as Stallmeister. Those who know Berolingen and its unique Thiergarten will, of course, not need to be told that the famous central avenue leading from the Brandenberg Gate in a straight line through the forest to Carolinenburg possesses one of the finest riding rows in all Europe. It was here that the young Princess, usually accompanied by one of her ladies, took her regular morning canter. On the occasion I speak of, it being a somewhat raw and threatening March day, the thoroughfare was almost deserted. Riders on the row there were practically none, and, apart from the few gapers whose attention was arrested by the ducal livery of the groom following us, and who stood still and stared as we passed, we could scarcely have enjoyed greater privacy had we been taking exercise in the palace grounds.

I was riding pensively about thirty yards behind the Princess and her lady, having fallen back in order to give some instructions to the groom, when suddenly a loud shriek burst upon my ear and caused me to start and look up. The shriek proceeded from the Princess's lady, and a glance was sufficient to satisfy me as to its cause. A man, who had apparently emerged from the forest that flanked the riding row, had seized the Princess's horse by the bridle, and was forcing the animal backwards with his right hand, whilst his left hand was raised towards her in an attitude of urgent supplication. The fellow, as I could easily discern from the distance, was speaking to her rapidly and with great earnestness, but what the import of his words was, it was, of course, impossible for me to distinguish. As I drove the spurs into my horse and galloped forward, I saw the Princess raise her riding-whip aloft, as if to strike at her assailant, and then lower her arm again without executing her purpose. The next instant the man's left arm shot forward, an object like a letter or paper of some description passed from his hand to that of the Princess, and, before I could quite realise what was occurring, he had released the bridle of the horse and disappeared with one or two bounds into the forest.

Something like an electric shock passed through me as I saw him vanish, for just at that moment my eye had fallen upon his uplifted arm, and I observed that *the forefinger of his left hand was missing.* I was near enough to recognise that the loss of the finger was of recent date, a circumstance that exercised my mind greatly and increased my desire to capture the fellow.

But here was a dilemma. Owing to the somewhat rough usage the Princess's horse had been subjected to, it had become restive, and, unnerved as its rider was by what had occurred, I could see that she was fast losing control of it. Indeed, almost before I had time to reflect whether I should spring to her assistance or follow my man into the wood, the spirited animal took a sudden side-leap and darted off at a furious gallop down the avenue. In an instant I had given my own horse the reins and was hot in pursuit. Hopeless as the attempt seemed, I had a notion that if I could overtake the affrighted beast before it reached the end of the avenue, which was fully two miles distant, I should succeed in seizing its bridle and checking its mad career. For the first minute or two I scarcely lessened the distance between us by a couple of yards. Then, however, thanks to the unstinted application of spurs and whip, I began to gain upon the fugitive very perceptibly, and, within a hundred yards or so of the main thorough-fare which crosses the avenue near the Imperial summer palace at the end, I came up with it.

But I was now confronted with a difficulty I had not reckoned upon. I had foolishly approached on the left side of the Princess, and consequently found myself unable to bring my animal near enough to reach over and seize the bridle of the runaway. I could have cursed myself for a senseless fool, but there was no time to dwell upon my folly. We were now barely fifty yards from the crossing, and in another minute would dash into the midst of the traffic passing there.

Riding neck and neck as we were, I could see that the Princess in her fright had lost all power over her limbs, and merely retained her seat owing to the fact that the course of her animal's flight was perfectly straight. The slightest swerve of the horse to the right or the left would have unseated her, with probably fatal consequences. The sweat stood out on my brow in great drops, as I realised the imminent peril of the situation. There was only one possible course to pursue, and, desperate though it was, I decided upon it instantly. Wrapping my own horse's bridle firmly round my left hand, I extended my right arm towards the half inanimate girl.

"Courage, Princess," I cried to her. "Rise in your stirrups and lean over towards me. I will answer for your safety."

I feared that she was already past comprehending me, but to my relief she obeyed mechanically, and, bending over until my body formed an obtuse angle with my beast, I clasped my arm tightly round her waist, and lifted her bodily on to my own saddle. The weight caused me to sway dangerously for a moment, and the fearful strain of the bridle in my left hand, as I simultaneously reined in my horse, nearly broke my wrist. But I maintained my balance with a supreme effort, and brought my beast to a standstill within half a dozen paces of the line of carriages and foot-passengers that was crossing the avenue at its lower end. Meanwhile the Princess's horse, relieved of its burden, turned sharply when it reached the crossing, and, retracing its course, careered back again towards the spot it had started from, where it was intercepted and caught by the groom.

I was a feat to be proud of, though I say it myself, who in my day have successfully matched my skill in similar *tours de force* against many a famous circus rider in his own arena. Still, but for the nerve displayed by my illustrious young mistress, I could not have accomplished it.

As her beautiful, lithe form lay closely nestled in my embrace, a thrill of immense pride and pleasure passed through me, and it was with difficulty that I restrained myself from caressing her. To escape the curiosity of the passers-by, who were attracted by the novel sight, I cantered back a couple of hundred yards, where I gently lifted my fair burden to the ground, and, dismounting myself, led her to a seat under the trees. She was still pale and trembling, but perfectly collected, and by the time her lady rode up and inquired tearfully whether she was injured, she had quite regained her old self again.

"I have had a jolly good fright, that's all," she said, in reply to her companion's question. "There's no need to make a fuss."

To me she had so far not addressed a word. But I had felt the warm pressure of her little hand that lay in mine as I conducted her to the seat, and it had spoken volumes. Now, however, she turned to me and said simply, in her delightful, unconventional little way—

"That was bravely done of you, Mr. Raleigh. You are a brick. I shall not forget it."

To convey on paper the sweet effect of her words and accent would lie impossible. There was as little sentimentality about her as there was stiffness or hauteur in her manner, and once her gratitude was expressed, the matter was dismissed for good. The groom had now trotted up with her Highness's horse, which she insisted on re-mounting, in spite of my remonstrances and the agonised entreaties of her lady that she would allow a carriage to be sent for and drive back to the palace.

"Nonsense, Wenzlau," she said, addressing the noble Fräulein somewhat peremptorily. "Do you take me for a hysterical schoolgirl? You may go home in a carriage if you prefer it; but when I ride out on horseback, I return on horseback or not at all."

I ventured to propose that, for safety's sake, we should exchange horses, and offered to transfer the saddle from her horse to mine. But she persisted in her determination to ride home on her own animal, and, having satisfied myself that there was no real danger, I assisted her to mount, and we returned to the city.

1 have noticed, in my humble experience of life, that the events of our existence which raise us, so to speak, to the summit of delight, are generally in the closest proximity to those which hurl us into the dust of shame and despondency. As I rode at the side of my young Princess, carefully watching every movement of her horse, I would not have exchanged my position for a generalship. Yet, before we reached the palace I was destined to meet with a rebuff that dashed my dearest hopes to the ground.

It occurred thus. Our little cavalcade had hardly issued from the avenue, and was crossing the large open space fronting the Arch of

Victory, or Brandenburg Gate, when the beating of drums and the sharp, regular clash of military arms close by indicated that the guard stationed behind the Arch had turned out and was rendering a royal salute. In another instant the carriage of the Emperor came into view, driving rapidly through the great arched gateway and across the square towards the Thiergarten.

Observing our little party, his Majesty immediately gave a sign for the carriage to be stopped, and the Princess rode forward to greet its Imperial occupant. The moment was an exciting one for me, for I could see by the animated way in which her Highness was conversing that she had plunged impulsively into a description of her recent adventure, and, from the quick glance which his Majesty once or twice shot in my direction, I judged that my own exploit bad not been passed over in silence.

I was just wondering whether the Princess would mention the circumstance of the paper handed to her by her strange assailant—a subject on which she had so far maintained complete silence—when I suddenly saw the Emperor beckon to me to approach. I went forward with a beating heart. I had never seen his Majesty at close quarters, and my natural curiosity, coupled with the elation I felt at being presented to him under what I thought such exceptionally favourable circumstances, caused me a mingled sensation of pride and nervous dread.

Judge of my consternation, then, when his Majesty, without waiting for the Princess to present me to him, and regarding me with a look of stern displeasure, addressed me as follows:—

"These are strange things I hear, Mr. Stallmeister. A princess attacked in my capital in open daylight before your eyes, without so much as an attempt being made to secure the guilty scoundrel. Is it the custom of gentlemen in your country to suffer such affronts to go unpunished?"

I began to stammer a few words of excuse, but his Majesty instantly cut me short.

"Are you not acquainted with the Arminian language?" he asked, speaking, as he had done before, in that tongue.

I replied that I was, though I could boast but of a poor scholarship.

"Then please to note, sir," his Majesty said curtly, "that it behoves the servant of an Arminian Princess to address the Arminian Emperor in the Arminian tongue."

This last shaft routed me utterly, and I stood there like a fool, quite at a loss for words to defend myself. The manifest injustice of this treatment, seeing that the Emperor had just been fully acquainted with the true circumstances of the occurrence which was apparently the cause of it, struck me less than what seemed to me to be the pointed animosity of the tone in which he addressed me. The Princess had noticed both with evident displeasure, and I saw her pretty lip pout ominously.

"I fear I have not explained myself clearly, sire," she said boldly, before I could collect myself to reply. "Doubtless Mr. Raleigh could have made an attempt to seize the man; but in that case it would certainly not have fallen to my lot to relate the facts of my adventure to your Majesty."

"I understand, I understand," the Emperor answered, totally ignoring the drift of her words, and still speaking with some irritability. "Rest assured, Princess, that the matter shall be strictly inquired into. My police shall leave no stone unturned to discover the perpetrator of this gross insult and bring him to justice. I will concern myself personally in the investigation."

"May I be permitted to state, sire," I now ventured to say, my confidence being somewhat restored by the generous intervention of my fair champion, "that the fellow has the forefinger of his left hand missing, and that I have reason to believe that it was cut off within the last four or five weeks."

I saw his Majesty give a slight start, and looked at me sharply.

"It is well," he said after a pause. "You will have an opportunity of giving such information as you may possess to the proper authorities."

He waved his hand in token that both the subject and I were dismissed, and, turning to the Princess, conversed with her for a few minutes, after which he saluted her Highness and drove on.

I think one is never more conscious of the intensity of one's hopes than at the moment when they crumble into dust. The manifest disfavour shown me by the Dowager Empress had led me to the conclusion that I should be the more likely to find grace with her imperious son. Yet, unaccountably enough, I had been received here with even greater coldness and repugnance. The mystery of it all was the greater that I could not imagine my present position had been secured to me without some favour in exalted quarters. Herr von Retzow, powerful though he was, could scarcely have placed me where I was unless he had been aided by others more influential than he. Who, then, were these? I had learned by this time to know that there were but two parties at the Imperial Court—that of the Emperor himself and that of his mother the Empress Fritz.

By those in whose midst I now lived I was supposed to be in the service of the former. Yet, if all the gossip I heard around me was true, the famous political spy, whom so many feared, had cast in his lot with tire Emperor's opponents, and was using the knowledge he possessed to paralyse the actions of those upon whom the success of his Majesty's pet schemes mainly depended. Surely a more puzzling situation could hardly he conceived.

The occurrence of that day seemed to me momentous enough to be made the subject of a special report to my patron, and I consequently repaired to his house towards midnight, the hour he had set for my visits, in order to place him in possession of the facts.

He received me, as he always did, with that curious mixture of kindly regard and conscious superiority which marked his whole bearing towards me. Inwardly I resented the tone of raillery he frequently fell into when addressing me. But there was that about the man which checked any expression of ill-humour on my part, and, to put it quite plainly, awed me into a state of sub-missiveness which often caused me to wonder at myself.

I offer this as an explanation of much that may appear dubious in the course of conduct I pursued towards a personage whose plans were then as much a mystery to me as he was himself. I would also, in justice to myself, beg the reader to understand that the Herr von Retzow, as he figured some weeks later in the famous political trial that engrossed the attention of Europe—as the convicted traitor and notorious blackmailer who levied fortunes by way of hush-money from those whose secrets he had made his own—was not the Herr von Retzow as he was known to the public at the time I am writing of. Else, on my word as a man arid a soldier, this history had never been penned.

Apart from the natural desire for my own preferment, I had had two strong personal reasons for entering the household of the Duchess of Bieberstein, conscious though I was that I did so practically in the capacity of a spy and an eavesdropper. In the first place, unless Herr von Retzow had grossly deceived me, it was in these surroundings that I was most likely to meet and identify the gentleman who had so narrowly missed knifing me that night in the Thiergarten six weeks ago; and, secondly, I knew of no better means of bringing about an encounter between my humble person and the illustrious Duke whom I had to thank, either directly or indirectly, for the present damaged condition of my cranium. I had vowed that I would not quit Arminian soil before I had crossed swords with his High-and-mightiness, for, with all due honour to royal blood, when it comes to hard knocks all the world is a level plain to me, and one skull as good as another.

Herr von Retzow listened to my story with rapt attention, but expressed no surprise.

"I cannot complain of the manner in which you have acquitted yourself," he said when I had finished, "save in one respect. The opportunity to secure the person of my particular friend with the missing forefinger was, I admit, forfeited through no fault of yours. But if you could not lay hands on the man himself, you might well have secured the next most important thing—namely, the paper he passed into the hands of the Princess. Did you not think of that while she lay unconscious in your very arms?"

The thing had certainly not occurred to me; nor, indeed, had it done so, would I have considered the act one worthy of an honourable man and a gentleman—a fact which I conveyed to my questioner in very plain terms.

"You are somewhat punctilious, my good friend, for a man in your position," he said, with that confounded air of a grand seigneur which he was wont to assume on occasions. "There is such a thing as a man proving too large for his boots, which is rather awkward when the boots happen to be purchased but not paid for. Nay, you need not grow angry," he added quietly, seeing me start up and redden at the taunt. "I know what I am saying, and you may believe me that you would have served the Princess more effectively by acting as I have suggested. But let that pass. On the whole, friend Sir Walter, I think I would rather entrust my safety to your sword than to your wit."

He was full of these cutting sayings; but he uttered them so coolly and so obviously unconscious of the possibility of their giving offence, that it was difficult to receive them otherwise than in good part. It was evident that he regarded the letter incident as being of more serious import than I had imagined. Indeed, he questioned me so closely as to what I knew of the Princess's movements and the opportunities afforded her for interviews with strangers that I concluded he anticipated some sinister design upon her person; and, my mind running, as it frequently did of late, upon the Duke of Friedrichsburg and his madcap escapades, I somewhat foolishly exclaimed that if it were he who contemplated any violence to her Highness, there was a certain person not too distantly connected with myself who would make him pay dearly for it.

Herr von Retzow looked at me with a glance of amused surprise.

"Oho!" he said, "you aim at high game, it appeal's. It would be well for you to remember, however, that we are not in England, and that there are such things as indictments for high treason in this country."

"Treason or no treason," I replied stubbornly, "I have an old score to settle with the Duke, and the opportunity shall not fail me for want of the making."

"Well," observed Herr von Retzow sardonically, "I am not sure that his Highness might not be the better for a little bloodletting. But let this jest go no further," he broke off sternly. "For one who aspires to win the Emperor's favour, you are venturing upon very dangerous ground."

"Pooh!" I said; "such threats do not frighten me. Truth to say, I would part with my chance of gaining his Majesty's good will for a mighty small consideration. It appears I am not of the make that pleases his Imperial fancy."

"Possibly because his Majesty knows more of Mr. Raleigh and his doings than Mr. Raleigh wots of," Herr von Retzow remarked drily.

His words made me start, recalling to my mind, as they did, the various whisperings I had lately heard of this man's daring interference in the political movements of the time. But before I could reply Herr von Retzow burst into a boisterous laugh.

"As I have said, my dear Sir Walter," he cried, "whatever your other abilities may be, you are decidedly lacking in detective penetration, or you would not be so blind to what is most obvious."

Saying which, he dismissed me in his usual peremptory fashion, after having cautioned me to note carefully who approached my young mistress, outside of those who formed her ordinary surroundings, and to inform him instantly of any unusual event that might occur in the ducal household.

I little dreamed how soon I should have occasion to follow these directions, nor how miserably I myself was to become involved in the extraordinary event which shortly befell, and which threw the whole court of Berolingen into a state of consternation.

It was about four days after my visit to Herr von Retzow, and three days before the famous masked ball that took place that year at the Imperial Palace—the first of its kind, I was told, ever given at the Arminian court—when the Princess Alexandrine sent for me early one morning, and, placing a strip of paper in my hands, asked me if I was acquainted with the address written upon it, and would undertake to conduct her thither.

"I intend to ride to this place within half an hour," she said, "accompanied by you and Wenzlau, whom I know I can trust. You will, therefore, have to find some excuse for leaving Friedrich (her Highness's groom) behind. The visit, I need hardly tell you, must be kept strictly secret."

I gave a glance at the paper, and fell back aghast. The address it contained was that of the identical house I had watched and entered that fatal night when I made the attempt to secure the mysterious packet of papers for Herr von Retzow.

"I am only too well acquainted with this place, Princess," I stammered at last. "If I may venture to advise your Highness—"

"No, you may not, Mr. Raleigh," she interrupted me in her most peremptory fashion. "I only take advice when I ask for it. You need feel no alarm," she added reassuringly. "I know my own mind, and am very well able to take care of myself."

With that she intimated to me very clearly that my interview was at an end, and I retired in a state of considerable perplexity.

What could I do? Had I refused to become a party to the expedition, it would undoubtedly have taken place without me, and what would have been gained thereby? It required little reflection to tell me that this proposed visit of the Princess to the house in the Waldstrasse was the sequel of her adventure in the Thiergarten four days before. Nor was its purpose any less easy of conjecture. What cared I, then, if the Princess, as appeared more than likely, were going there to obtain proofs, as I had obtained them, of the Duke of Friedrichsburg's secret marriage? At all events, I could not prevent it. My sense of justice and propriety had always rebelled at the thought of the projected union between this sweet girl and the notorious rake who was bound by every instinct of truth and honour, if not by the law itself, to abide by his sacred pledge to another. I knew, of course, that no alliance entered into by a member of the Arminian Imperial family is regarded as binding in law, unless it be contracted with the express sanction of the head of the reigning house. But I knew also, just as surely, that if the Princess Alexandrine once learned of such an alliance on the part of Duke Ernest, no power on earth would induce her to confer her hand upon him, let the law say what it might.

When her Highness started out, therefore, about half an hour later, on this peculiar expedition, I accompanied her with some misgivings as to the view Herr von Retzow might take of my ready compliance with her wishes, but certainly without the slightest apprehension that any danger threatened her person.

In order to avoid the main thoroughfares and the public attention our appearance there was sure to attract, we took a round-about course to our destination, passing eastward through the quiet residential quarter in the rear of the museums and picture galleries. It was consequently fully three-quarters of an hour before we reached the house in the Waldstrasse.

While I assisted the Princess to dismount at the front gate, where she directed ns to await her return, I glanced curiously up the drive at the windows of the house, secretly wondering what kind of an interview was about to take place there, and whether my erstwhile charmer from Wittichau in Silesia would have any part in it. As I did so, the face of a man appeared for the space of an instant at one of the upper windows, and vanished again immediately. Brief as that instant was, however, it had given me an opportunity to scan the man's features, and, incredible though it seemed, I could have sworn they were those of Herr von Retzow himself.

A good deal disturbed by this coincidence, if coincidence it was, I would have asked the Princess's permission to accompany her at least to the entrance of the house, where I should be closer at hand in case of need, but she anticipated my intention before I could carry it out, and, forbidding me in almost stern terms to follow her beyond the gate, walked with rapid strides alone up the drive-way to the house door. I saw it open at her approach, and noted with a sense of relief that the person who received her Highness was a woman. The door closed, however, too quickly to allow of my recognising who it was.

I passed the minutes that now followed in a state of anxious suspense, which grew in intensity as I gradually conjured up in my mind all the possible dangers to which my young mistress might be exposed. The certainty that the man whose face I had seen appear at the window was Herr von Retzow, while it mystified me beyond description, caused me no particular alarm in itself. That this Herr von Retzow was an inveterate schemer I had good reason to know. But from my experience of him I believed him to be, if not an absolutely honourable and scrupulous gentleman, at least one who would be incapable of ensnaring and doing injury to an innocent and defenceless girl. The very daring of such a thing, in face of the fact, of which he was now doubtless aware, that the Princess had not come unprotected, made it seem impossible to conceive.

Yet, as twenty minutes, and even a half hour passed without sign of her Highness's return, my uneasiness became a veritable torture. She bad assured me that her presence in the house would not exceed a quarter of an hour. What, then, could be detaining her there? I saw that Fräulein von Wenzlau herself had now grown alarmed, and, determined at all cost to satisfy myself of the Princess's safety, I tied my horse to a tree, and, walking up the drive to the house, knocked resolutely at the door. Receiving no response, I knocked again, this time with such vigour that the possibility of the sound not being heard inside was out of the question. But all remained still. I listened through the keyhole—for the door, upon my trying it, proved to be locked—but I heard no sound save the thumping of my own heart against my breast. To all appearances the place was totally deserted.

Roused now to a pitch of frenzied fear, I hammered against the door with both my fists until they were so much bruised that the continuance of the operation caused me actual pain. Then I bethought myself of another and more effective mode of procedure. I had entered the house once before by unusual means, and what was to prevent me from doing so again now? Banning round to the verandah fronting the garden proper, I swung myself upon it, and smashing in the first window I reached, crept through the aperture thus created, and so effected my entrance into the house.

The room I entered was the same one that I had been in on the occasion of my former adventure. But it was empty, and passing through it into the outer passage I rushed at breakneck speed through the entire house, entering room after room, and searching every nook and corner, even down to the kitchen and cellar, without finding a living soul anywhere. The place was completely deserted.

I rubbed my eyes and forehead in my utter perplexity to account for the strange fact. But no amount of thinking and speculating could alter it. The Princess was gone, and those she had come to visit, whoever they were, had disappeared with her. Had she been kidnapped, murdered, abducted, or what? I could have kicked myself, as I stood there actually wringing my hands in my desperation, for the incredible folly I had been guilty of in permitting my young mistress to enter such a place unaccompanied.

In the fever of my anxiety I recommenced my investigation and went through the house once more from the top to the bottom, but to no purpose, so far as the object I had in view was concerned, which was to find the Princess. My search this time, however, was rewarded by a discovery which at least threw some light on her Highness's strange disappearance, though it was far from affording any explanation of its cause. There was a kitchen door, as I now found, leading into a kind of back garden, at the end of which I could see a hedge that evidently divided the garden from a narrow lane beyond, for while I was gazing through one of the latticed windows in the basement I saw the head of some passer-by appeal above the hedge in the distance, indicating clearly that there was some kind of thoroughfare behind it.

The discovery acted upon me like a charm. Doubtless there was a gate leading from the garden to the lane, and if the Princess had left the house by this back exit, whether of her own free will or under compulsion, I might possibly still overtake her. Without a moment's delay, therefore, I hastened back to the spot where I had tied up my horse, and bidding the Princess's lady, who had by this time arrived at a state of tearful imbecility, await my return, I mounted the beast and rode off at a gallop.

Taking the first left turning I came to, I struck the lane, as I had calculated, within about fifty yards of the spot where it passed the garden hedge. But, unfortunately, its whole length, as I now perceived, did not exceed three or four hundred yards, and, what was worse, though it had but one outlet, being a kind of blind alley, this communicated with an important thoroughfare, amidst the bustle and traffic of which it was all but hopeless to track the fugitives. Still, I persevered for a while, riding up the street about half a mile in each direction, and inquiring in vain of every constable I met whether he had seen any persons pass by answering to the description I was able to give. At last, feeling that further pursuit was futile, and only meant a loss of valuable time, I returned once more to the place where I had left Fräulein von Wenzlau, and telling her in a few brief words what had happened, requested her to accompany me with all speed back to the palace in order to notify the Dowager Duchess of her daughter's strange disappearance.

Instead of responding to my request, however, the brainless girl promptly went off into a violent fit of hysterics, which threatened to detain us still longer, for I was totally at sea as to how I ought to act in such an emergency. In my rage I fortunately applied by instinct what I have since learned is the best remedy in cases of this kind, that is to say, I gave the girl a sound rating, winding up with the threat that I would hand her over to the next policeman for safe custody, and proceed alone to the ducal palace, unless she instantly stopped her tomfoolery and accompanied me.

The effect was instantaneous. She called me a brute of an Englishman, whose company no Arminian lady of noble birth ought to be forced to endure, and rode off at such a pace that I had no little difficulty in keeping up with her. But the main object was gained, for in another twenty minutes we had reached the palace, where, the Duchess being absent, I unfolded my tale to the Master of the Household, with the result that, in less time than it takes me to write it down, the entire establishment was in a state of indescribable confusion and uproar.

Mounted grooms were sent off in every direction, the Prefect of Police was immediately summoned to the palace, and messengers were despatched to the Minister of the Interior—the Arminian equivalent of our Home Secretary—asking for the adoption of prompt measures to ensure the safety and the ultimate restoration of the kidnapped Princess.

In the midst of all this turmoil and disorder, I quietly took my leave, and, jumping into a droschky, directed the driver to take me at his top speed to the residence of Herr von Retzow. I was determined, in the first place, to make sure, without loss of time, that I had been mistaken in his supposed identity with the personage whose face I had seen at the window of the house in the Waldstrasse, and, secondly, provided I really found him at his place of abode, to acquaint him with the startling event of that morning, and enlist Iris aid in searching for the lost Princess.

It had struck the half hour after noon when I arrived at the well-known house, which I had, until then, never visited except at night. The door was opened by a servant in dark blue livery, whose face was unknown to me, and who, upon my inquiry whether Herr von Retzow was within, regarded me with a stare of supercilious surprise.

"There is no person of that name living here," he said curtly. "You have probably mistaken the house."

"Not at all," I answered. "I have visited Herr von Retzow here on several occasions. But I am not particular about the name. If your master is within, you will be good enough to announce me to him. I am Mr. Walter Raleigh, Master of the Horse to her Serene Highness the Duchess of Bieberstein."

I knew the Arminian weakness for high-sounding titles, and had not miscalculated the effect of my words.

"I am very sorry, sir," the man said civilly, "but there must be some mistake in the address. This house belongs to his Excellency Colonel Heinrich von Stauffenberg."

"Very well, then, if the Colonel is within," I said quickly, "have the goodness to conduct me to him. I have matters of importance to communicate to him."

I spoke on the spur of the moment, without consideration. I had often seen Colonel von Stauffenberg these last few weeks, and was aware that he and the man I knew as Herr von Retzow were two quite different persons. I knew, moreover, that his Excellency was a stern and uncompromising follower of the Emperor, who was as little likely to associate on intimate terms with a man like von Retzow as I was likely to fraternise with a cowherd. It afforded me, therefore, almost a sense of relief when the servant answered—

"But his Excellency is not within. He is on duty"—meaning in attendance on the Emperor—"and will not return home for three or four days. Of course, if you desire that a message be delivered to his Excellency—"

"No, no," I said hastily; "that is unnecessary."

In fact, I was at that moment in a state of confusion that left me very much in doubt whether my head was still between my shoulders or floating about in some other unknown region. The unexpected denial of Herr von Retzow's connection with this house, where I had seen him act as undisputed master, the recollection of the face at the window in the Waldstrasse, of whose true identity I was now more than ever convinced; in short, the whole string of strange contradictions which appeared to characterise the actions of the extraordinary personage who, for more than six weeks, had exercised a controlling influence over my destiny, excited my imagination to such a degree that I felt as if I were in the hands of some uncanny power, and, stammering a foolish excuse, I fairly turned tail and fled, no doubt leaving the pompous lacquey fully convinced that he had been dealing with an escaped lunatic.

As I entered the Wilhelmstrasse, ten minutes afterwards, from the Avenue of Limes, the Emperor's carriage, preceded by two mounted policemen, and driving almost at a gallop, turned into the street at the same time. His Majesty's looks, of which I just caught a glimpse as the carriage whirled by, were as black as thunder, and he paid no response whatever to the respectful salutations of the people, who stopped and uncovered as their Emperor swept past them. From the direction the carriage was taking, and other significant circumstances, I guessed without difficulty that his Majesty's destination was the ducal palace, and desirous, for obvious reasons, to avoid approaching the Imperial presence just now, I altered my course, and, instead of returning to the palace at once, as I had intended, proceeded to my lodgings, where I spent a couple of hours in distracted meditation before venturing back to the scene of my duties.

When I reached the palace at last, towards four in the afternoon, order had to some extent been restored there, but no clue to the whereabouts of the young Princess had as yet been found. Nor, indeed, was the diligent search prosecuted by the authorities during the next few days rewarded by one particle of success. Not a trace of the lost Princess Alexandrine of Bieberstein could be found. She had disappeared, it seemed, as completely as if the earth had swallowed her up.

As for myself, a perusal of the following missive will enable the reader to judge for himself of my condition of mind at this juncture. It was delivered at the palace by an ordinary street messenger about half an hour after my return, and ran as follows:—

> "You are a sad simpleton, my dear Sir Walter. I can only hope that you will still retrieve some of the confidence I have reposed in you. We may meet again three days hence at the Imperial court ball, which you will attend without fail. My further instructions will reach you there.—H. v. R."

To say that this message, which in its cool insolence capped everything else I had experienced during the last six weeks, completely staggered me, would be putting it too mildly. I was furious at the assumption of authority which its contents argued, but I was also totally nonplussed by its general tenor. That Herr von Retzow had had a hand in the abduction of the Princess Alexandrine was a fact I could have all but sworn to in a court of law. Yet, unless I was unable to read English aright, here was this same Herr von Retzow upbraiding me for not having prevented that calamity.

It was worse than useless, however, to cogitate upon the subject, for the more I tried to fit the pieces of the puzzle together, the more intricate it seemed to grow. Moreover, I soon had matters nearer home to engross my thoughts.

That evening I received a verbal notification from Baron von Brinkwitz curtly dismissing me from my office in the ducal household. It was a grievous blow to me, of course; still, it was not an unexpected one, and I received it with a certain amount of equanimity.

I was now once more a free lance, with little prospect of ever again intervening in the destiny of a Princess of the house of Bieberstein, or of even attending an Imperial masked ball.

That I felt deeply humiliated by this new change in my fortunes goes without saying. But the humiliation was agreeably tempered with a sense of satisfaction at my release from a thraldom which had commenced to gall me, and when I laid my head upon my pillow that night I did so with the solemn vow that no man on earth should again induce me to take upon myself the anxieties and responsibilities I was now quit of.

Better men than I have made similar vows before now, and broken them in spite of themselves, as I shortly broke mine. But this belongs to a new story.

THE INCIDENT OF THE PRINCESS
IN DISGUISE AND THE CONSPIRACY
IN THE HOSTELRY AT WITTICHAU

WITTICHAU is a small garrison town of about fifty thousand inhabitants on the borders of Silesia. It is situated at a distance of about two hundred and fifty miles from Berolingen, and lies upon the direct railway route between that city and the Austrian capital.

I would spare the reader these dry geographical statistics but for the fact that, by what I have always considered one of the strangest coincidences in my career, this place now became the scene of events so startling in character that it can scarcely be wondered at if in their sequel I was induced to cast all my good resolves to the four winds and enter once more upon the course of strange adventure which I had vowed to abandon.

Perhaps some may consider that I already partly broke that vow by repairing to Wittichau at all, which I did the second night after my dismissal from the Bieberstein household. My object, however, was not the search of adventure, but merely the gratification of a very natural desire to learn the true facts regarding the alleged marriage of the woman who had tricked me so shamefully seven or eight months before.

The means of obtaining light on this point appeared very simple, for I reckoned that, if what she had told me that night of my adventure in the house in the Waldstrasse were true, I should find a leaf in the Wittichau register of marriages missing, and in that event could consider her story established. Unfortunately, I did not reckon that my polite request to be allowed to inspect the register would be met with a surly negative on the part of the official entrusted with the safe-keeping of these important records; and, as this proved to be the case, I saw the success of my quest barred at the outset by an insuperable obstacle.

So much, then, for the innocence of my purpose in going to Wittichau and my failure to obtain the knowledge I desired. The knowledge I did obtain there proved to be of a different description altogether, and was certainly not of my seeking. But the facts shall speak for themselves.

I had taken up my quarters at a well-known roadside tavern or hostelry, about two miles from Wittichau proper, which possessed a certain interest in my eyes from the fact of its having once harboured beneath its roof the famous hero of the Seven Years' War—the great warrior king who may be said to have prepared, if not laid, the foundation of Arminia's present greatness. In the garden of this ancient hostelry, appropriately christened "Zum Alten Fritz," I was nursing my disappointment at the failure of my expedition early in the afternoon after my arrival in Wittichau, when my mind was suddenly diverted from the thoughts of my personal affairs by an incident which set my curiosity agog in quite a new direction.

It was a lovely spring day, and I had ensconced myself, fortified with a bottle of choice Rhine wine, in an arbour at the lower end of the garden, to deliberate on my next move. Possibly the warmth of the afternoon sun, which shone almost unhindered through the scarcely-developed foliage of the creeper growing up the lattice-work of the arbour, or, more likely still, the wine I had drunk, exercised a soporific effect upon me. At any rate, I fell into a quiet slumber, from which I was awakened by the sound of voices close by.

The persons conversing appeared to be sauntering to and fro on the short pathway running along the hedge at the end of the garden, for their voices rose and fell at regular intervals, enabling me only to catch disjointed snatches of their discourse. That this latter was of a nature to interest me and justify my playing the *rôle* of an eavesdropper will be conceded by the most scrupulous of men when I state that its subject was no less a personage than his Majesty the Emperor Willibald of Arminia, and that one of the two individuals engaged in it, incredible as it may sound in view of the humble surroundings I am speaking of, was a person of scarcely inferior rank. At least, no other supposition was possible, unless I were to assume that some absurd farce was being enacted for my especial delectation, for the first words that reached my ear upon my awaking were these—

"I can assure your Royal Highness that there are not ten physicians of repute in Berolingen who would not cheerfully confirm the testimony I am prepared to give regarding his Majesty's lamentable mental derangement. If I have attached somewhat rigorous conditions to the rendering of that testimony, I beg your Royal Highness to believe that I am not actuated by any mercenary motives in doing so. In my position as body physician to his Majesty I shall naturally be exposed to certain risks, which—"

"I fully understand your motives, Doctor," the other here broke in, in a tone which I thought had a touch of contempt in it; "we need not discuss this further. The compensation you are to receive for such services as you may have to render is a matter I leave you to settle with others who are more conversant with these things. You would oblige me, however by dropping the formal appellation you are good enough to bestow upon me. While I am here I am plain Herr Leopold, and would beg you to treat and address me accordingly."

They passed out of my hearing at this point, and by the time they again came within earshot the drift of their conversation had altered. Evidently the chief personage Herr Leopold, as he dubbed himself, had come there to meet had not kept his appointment, and his disgust at being kept waiting found vent in frequent strong exclamations of impatience.

"If he should play us false," I heard him say angrily, "he shall pay dearly for it." And, again—"This matter must be consummated before another week has passed; there are too many interests involved, and further delay may bring premature disclosure. Why is he not here? His non-appearance is, to say the least, very suspicious. I don't like the man's reputation—I don't like the man's reputation!"

He repeated this last sentiment several times, but I could gather nothing further of the personage referred to, excepting that he was, according to the assurance of the individual I had heard addressed as "Doctor," detained upon some other important business with the particulars of which the doctor was not acquainted.

Needless to say, I was by this time on the tip-toe of excited curiosity, and strained my ears to the utmost to catch some further scraps of their conversation. But it was evident that, failing the presence of the principal agent in the conspiracy of which I had so accidentally obtained a general outline, the illustrious guest of mine host of the "Alter Fritz" felt disinclined to talk. Indeed, he presently notified his intention of retiring to his room in the hostelry, where he would await the arrival of the third party to the conference, and, after exchanging a few more remarks, the two men sauntered away again in the direction of the house.

I waited until the sound of their retreating footsteps was lost in the distance, and then emerged from my place of concealment in a state of considerable perturbation. What I had heard was plainly a plot to depose and possibly incarcerate His Majesty the Emperor Willibald on the plea of lunacy. But, having heard it, what was I to do with it? It was impossible to say who else might not be implicated in this nefarious design, for, as all the world knows, his somewhat eccentric Majesty's reign, though a subject of unmingled satisfaction to himself, had not been so to everybody else, and to assess the number of those who would have joyfully endorsed the physician's certificate as to his mental incapability would entail work almost assuming the dimensions of a census.

One thing I felt certain of. It was not likely that a plan of this far-reaching character would have been seriously considered unless the co-operation of men nearer the Imperial throne than those whose conversation I had overheard had been first secured. Such danger, therefore, as was threatening the Emperor was obviously very imminent.

Could it be possible that Herr von Retzow, the astute detective who was supposed to hold in the palm of his hand the threads of all the political intrigues festering at the court of Berolingen, was ignorant of this strange conspiracy? It afforded me a sense of no little satisfaction to think that I was to be the means of acquainting him with these startling facts. Perhaps I should not have contemplated such a thing, after what I considered the shameful duplicity with which he had treated me in the matter of the abduction of the Princess of Bieberstein, had I known of any other channel through which I could have conveyed a warning to the Emperor. But I knew of no other, and, after all, though my faith in the perfect integrity of Herr von Retzow had been rather rudely shaken, I had no reason to harbour any doubts as to his loyalty to the sovereign whose interests he pretended to serve.

Deliberating on these matters, I returned to the inn and mounted the stairs to my room. The place was of pretty ancient origin, as was evidenced by the straggling nature of its structure, it having apparently been a good deal altered and added to at various dates during the course of its chequered existence. Situated as it was just at the junction of two very important highways, it had in former days done service as a convenient halting-place for travellers journeying by stage coach or otherwise to and from almost every part of the province. The railroads had long put an end to its profitable utility in this respect, but it still remained on the spot where it had stood for so many a year, unchanged externally, as a memento of the romantic old days which we now only read of in books, or sometimes still hear of, in their retrospective moods, from the lips of our grandfathers and grandmothers.

The room I had had assigned to me was situated in the main, and probably oldest, part of the building, and overlooked the entrance porch facing the high road to Wittichau. As I entered it I heard a carriage drive up at a rapid pace from the direction of the town and stop at the inn door. Impelled by curiosity to ascertain what kind of guest or guests it was bringing to mine host of the "Alter Fritz," and thinking I might possibly catch a glimpse of the gentleman whose lack of punctuality had so seriously displeased my unknown friend in the garden below, I stepped quickly to the window and looked out.

I was just in time to see the coat-tails of a man disappear into the house. But the carriage had not discharged all its freight. Two ladies now alighted and passed quickly into the hostelry. The one, a slim, girlish figure, wore a thick veil which completely hid her features. The other I recognised instantly as my former acquaintance of Wittichau, the mistress of the house in the Waldstrasse.

For a moment or two I remained at the window scarcely realising the full import of what I had seen. Then gradually something in the figure and carriage of the girl in the veil began to impress itself upon me as familiar, and my heart gave a great leap. Was it possible? Could this be the Princess Alexandrine? I gave myself no time to weigh the probability or improbability of her appearance here, at an obscure country inn some 250 miles from Berolingen, but, hastening from the room, made my way with all speed downstairs, where I hoped to intercept the newcomers before they were conducted to their room.

On reaching the ground floor I found no trace of the man, but the two ladies were crossing the lobby towards the staircase I had just descended. They were already within a few feet of me, when of a sudden my friend from Wittichau perceived me, and, seizing her companion by the arm, literally whisked her into a passage leading to the left wing of the house, at the end of which I knew there was a smaller stairway to the floor above.

Determined not to be so easily foiled, and now more certain than ever that the veiled lady was the Princess of Bieberstein, I followed as quickly as I could without exciting the attention of the idlers standing about in the lobby. The corridor was so dark that in rushing along it I was in imminent peril of breaking my neck; and, indeed, just as I arrived at the foot of the staircase I stumbled rather heavily against someone apparently approaching from the opposite direction. The person, whoever it was—for it was impossible to recognise his features in the dark passage—appeared to lose his equilibrium, and only saved himself from falling headlong by clutching me round the neck. I apologised hastily, and shaking myself free as soon as I could, continued on my way. But the consequence of the delay was that I only reached the top of the small stairway in time to see the objects of my pursuit vanish into one of the rooms on the first floor, slamming and locking the door behind them.

I stood for a moment irresolute. Should I knock and demand admission? My purpose might be misconstrued, and possibly land me in unpleasant difficulties, should the occupants of the room resent my intrusion.

I was still revolving the matter in my mind when I heard the heavy tread of a man ascending the stairs, and instinctively drew aside to wait until he came into view and I could ascertain who it was. I fancied now, as I thought of the occurrence a moment or two ago in the passage below, that the person who had collided so violently with me there had clung to me somewhat more tenaciously than the occasion called for, and I suspected some design in his action. The moment the individual I now heard approaching turned the corner at the top of the stairs I knew that my suspicion had been only too well founded. It was no other than Herr von Retzow himself.

I waited with breathless expectation to see what his next movement would be, feeling certain that he would proceed straight to the room I had just seen the ladies enter. Nor did I prove mistaken. Looking cautiously around him, apparently expecting to see me, he advanced a few steps along the passage in the direction of the room in question. His hand was already upon the handle of the door, and I was preparing to dart forward and enter with him, if necessary by force, when something entirely unexpected happened which altered the whole aspect of affairs.

It was the sudden appearance upon the scene of another personage, who now came hurrying along the passage towards the main staircase. As he caught sight of Herr von Retzow he stopped abruptly, and, addressing him by name, exclaimed—

"Why, here you are! Upon my soul, man, you have an enviable nerve. The Prince has been fretting and fuming like an overheated steam engine for the last half hour. If ho is kept waiting much longer, there will be the devil to pay."

Although I could not see the speaker, for his back was turned to me, I recognised his voice at once. It was that of the gentleman whose conversation with the mysterious stranger I had overheard in the garden of the hostelry that afternoon.

There was a moment's pause, then a muttered exclamation of impatience, half-suppressed, followed by an admonition to remember that even the walls of a country inn are liable to have ears, and the two men proceeded together down the passage towards the main staircase.

I issued from the recess in which I had concealed myself, hardly daring to trust the evidence of my own senses. So the personage Herr Leopold, as he called himself, had come here to meet was none other than Herr von Retzow himself, and I, idiot that I was, had been on the point of confiding the dangerous secret I had become possessed of to the very man whom it most nearly concerned.

The alarming nature of this discovery almost caused me to lose my interest in the Princess of Bieberstein and her detention in this obscure place; for that she was detained here against her will, and that Herr von Retzow had some hand in the business, was now a matter of settled conviction with me. After cudgelling my brains in vain to devise some means of obtaining an interview with the Princess, I decided to post myself at the entrance to the inn, where she was bound to pass me if she left the place again, which I had reason to suppose she would do shortly, seeing that the carriage she had come in was still waiting outside.

I found the lobby below now almost deserted, save for the presence of the landlord himself, a rather surly specimen of his genus, from whom I vainly endeavoured to extract some information regarding his strange guests. I believe the fellow had been warned against me or cautioned not to talk, for he received my inquiries with ill-concealed suspicion, and evidently regarded my continued presence in the lobby as an impertinent intrusion. I was not to be deterred from my purpose, however, by surly looks and rude insinuations, and only stuck all the more obstinately to my post. I had been there about an hour, and the shades of evening were already beginning to fall, when the two persons I had heard conversing in the garden came down the stairs, and, passing out of the house, walked away in the direction of the town.

Evidently the conference with Herr von Retzow had ended satisfactorily, for the countenance of the distinguished stranger wore an expression of contentment which had been absent from it before. But where was Herr von Retzow himself? Had he remained behind for some purpose of his own? And if so, for what purpose? I felt uneasy and at a loss what to do.

Presently I observed the driver of the carriage that had drawn up on the opposite side of the road touch up his horses and drive slowly away in the direction taken by the two strangers. The manner in which this occurred was such as to convince me that the man had obeyed a signal from the house, and I involuntarily suspected some devilry. For all I knew of the place and its surroundings, there might be some back entrance where the carriage could drive up unseen, in which case my good friends were likely to escape with their captive unobserved, while I was standing here like a fool watching an empty space.

The thought was no sooner conceived than I had made up my mind how to act. Deserting my post, therefore, I now made my way once more with all speed to the floor above, and, proceeding straight to the room where I had seen the Princess and her companion enter an hour or more before, I knocked boldly and demanded admission.

No answer came, however, and everything remained so still in the room that I could have almost doubted the possibility of any living soul being in it. I called through the keyhole, stating who I was, and asking the Princess to inform me if she were there of her own free will, in which case I would retire satisfied. But the result was the same. All remained quiet.

Exasperated at this persistent silence, I now brought my whole weight to bear upon the door, for I was determined to gain an entrance by fair means or foul. Thanks to the rottenness of the ancient woodwork, it yielded to the pressure at once, and, the door flying open, I all but tumbled headlong into the room.

To my surprise, I found that it was empty. There was an inner door in the side wail, however, which evidently led to an adjoining apartment, and, after trying it and finding it locked, I knocked loudly upon the panels. Although I received no answer, I could hear this time unmistakable sounds of someone moving on the other side. I therefore called out that unless the door were unlocked immediately I would burst it open. The threat appeared to have some effect, for a key was presently inserted in the lock on the other side, and the voice of a man called to me to have a moment's patience.

The person, whoever it was, fumbled some time with the lock, apparently without succeeding in turning the key. At last, in response to my impatient exclamations, he suggested that the door might he bolted on my side. I looked, but though there was a bolt on my side of the door, it was withdrawn, and, concluding that the fellow was playing a game with me to delay my admittance, I was just about to repeat my performance of a minute before, when I suddenly heard the click of the key turning in the lock, and the next moment the door was opened from the other side.

I rushed into the room, and saw myself face to face with Herr von Retzow. Not another soul was visible. Without waiting to exchange a word with him, I darted to the outer door of the room, but only to find it locked.

"May I ask," Herr von Retzow now inquired in a cold, harsh voice, "what is the meaning of this insolent intrusion?"

"The meaning is this," I exclaimed angrily; "that, unless you conduct me without an instant's delay to the presence of her Highness the Princess Alexandrine, I shall throttle you where you stand, and put an end to your rascally existence."

The words were scarcely out of my mouth when I heard the grating sound of carriage wheels in the distance; and, darting to the window, which overlooked a portion of the garden running parallel with the high road, I saw the conveyance I had been watching downstairs drive away at a rapid pace towards Wittichau, with the Princess and her companion inside.

I had been fooled. Doubtless the carriage I had seen drive off a few moments before had merely changed its position in obedience to a signal from the house. In all probability it had drawn up again at the garden gate a little further on, and the Princess had then been hurried downstairs and through the garden to the high road, whilst I was being kept parleying for admittance at the inner door connecting this apartment with the one I had first entered.

The ugly smile, full of triumphant malice, which flitted across Herr von Retzow's features as I turned away from the window and looked at him, tempted me sorely to carry out the threat I had uttered a few moments ago, and strangle the fellow there and then. But I wanted to obtain information regarding the destination of the Princess, and this would hardly have been the way to secure it. I restrained myself, therefore, for the time being, and, addressing my companion politely, told him in very plain words that I considered our compact at an end, and that, unless he complied with my demand, and took instant measures to deliver the Princess Alexandrine into my keeping, I would make matters uncommonly warm for him.

"You may think the game is entirely yours, my friend," I said quietly. "But I happen to possess a trump card which you have quite left out of the reckoning, and it will depend upon your next move whether I play it or not."

He made no answer, but stood regarding me as before with a grin of contemptuous amusement, as if I were some prattling idiot whose words it was not worth while to take seriously. I felt my choler rising, and continued in a tone of irony—

"To be more explicit, my precious Herr von Retzow, I have not passed the last six hours in this ramshackle old inn without ascertaining the full depth of your loyalty to the sovereign you pretend to serve, and I would advise you to consult both your interests and those of your friend, 'Herr Leopold,' before you defy the man who holds the fate of both of you in the palm of his hand."

This time I had hit straight home. The expression of the man's countenance changed instantly, and he turned pale as death.

"You fool of an Englishman!" he exclaimed suddenly, pointing with energy towards the window, "look out there."

The impressiveness of his tone and action startled me, and I stepped quickly to the window and looked out. As I did so I heard a low laugh behind me, and, turning round swiftly, saw Herr von Retzow disappear through the door leading to the adjoining apartment. With one bound I was across the room again, but not before he had closed the door and drawn the bolt on the other side, locking me in the room.

I rushed to the other door, which gave on to the passage, but it was locked too, and I was a prisoner. I threw myself with all my weight against it, thinking to burst it open as I had done the one of the adjoining room. But my efforts in this instance proved unavailing, and I had to desist. Nor was I more fortunate with the inner door. They both opened into the room I was confined in, and, consequently, no pressure from my side could make the locks yield.

"Fairly caught," I muttered to myself, feeling more ashamed at the easy way I had allowed myself to be duped than angry at the plight I found myself in. I had little leisure, however, to devote to thoughts of this description, for there now arose such a hubbub and noise in the hostelry below that I concluded Herr von Retzow had lost no time in informing the landlord of what had occurred, no doubt varnishing his tale to suit his own purposes.

As I listened I could hear the staircase creak in the distance under the tread of several pairs of feet. Presently there was a rush of people in the passage, a key was inserted in the lock, and the next instant Herr von Retzow appeared on the threshold accompanied by the landlord and two of the inn hands.

"I call upon you in the Emperor's name to arrest that man," he said, pointing to me. "He is a dangerous foreign anarchist."

Evidently the landlord was aware of his guest's calling, for he received his order in that peculiarly obsequious manner which is so eminently characteristic of the Arminian in his dealings with police officials. Motioning to his two assistants to follow him, he advanced a step or two into the room, and then came to an abrupt halt, trembling in every limb like an aspen leaf. He had good cause for this exhibition of fear, for I had quietly drawn my revolver and covered him with it.

"The first one who advances another step," I said, "will be a dead man. I have a bullet here for each of you, and a couple to spare."

I retreated backwards towards the open window as I spoke, and, lifting myself quickly on to the ledge, sat regarding my would-be captors with a look of defiance.

"Remember," I said, as I took a rapid survey of the height and the ground below, "the man who hinders or follows me takes his life in his hands. That villain there"—and I pointed my revolver at Herr von Retzow, whose right hand had made an ominous movement towards his breastpocket—"is a traitor to the Emperor whose name he misuses, and I warn you to beware of him."

With these words I vaulted quickly over the ledge and took a flying leap to the ground beneath. I was not a minute too soon, for a bullet whizzed so close by my head as I fell that I felt the hair on my crown stir as it passed. It was from Herr von Retzow's pistol, and I had hardly gathered myself up from the soft ground on which I had fallen and started to run for the hedge beyond which the open fields lay, when three more shots followed quickly one upon the other, each striking the earth within no great distance from me.

But the dusk had now deepened considerably, and it would have been the merest chance had I been struck. Once over the garden hedge, and I could defy all pursuit. It was an easy vault over, and a minute later I had gained the tract of potato field that stretched from the hedge to a small copse of hazelnut trees about half a mile distant.

It was my object to gain this cover with as little loss of time as possible. Not that I had any apprehension of being followed and captured. I would have matched myself at a foot race with the fleetest runner in all Arminia. But I thought it expedient to put myself out of my pursuers' sight as quickly as I could, and this was the best means that presented itself of doing so.

When I reached my goal at last I threw myself on the ground at the foot of a solitary birch tree, and proceeded to consider the situation. Had anyone, I thought to myself dolefully, ever experienced such vicissitudes of fortune within so short a time as I had since my arrival in Berolingen? I cursed the hour which had thrown me in the path of this villainous von Retzow, and I cursed my own folly in always casting myself incontinently into the breach for others who concerned me no more than did the man in the moon. For, after all, what interest had I in the fate of the Princess of Bieberstein, or, for the matter of that, in the sanity or insanity of his self-opinionated Majesty the Emperor Willibald of Arminia, whose incarceration as a lunatic, if permitted by his own people, would certainly be hailed by many outside of his dominions as a boon and a blessing to mankind? As for the wilful little Princess Alexandrine, I had some suspicion that she was herself not altogether free from participation in the trickery that had been played upon me that afternoon. It struck me at least as strange, now I thought the matter over calmly, that one so spirited as I knew her to be should submit so tamely to the coercion I had supposed her to be enduring.

At all events, I resolved to wash my hands henceforth of her and her fate, and proceeded to turn my thoughts to my own immediate future. My first consideration was how I was to get safely back to Berolingen; for return there I must, since all I possessed in the world was stored away in the old trunk I had left behind me in my lodgings. I had no doubt that Herr von Retzow, using his influence at police headquarters, would take prompt measures to have my person secured on my arrival in the capital. Unless, therefore, I was desirous of gaining some practical experience of the methods adopted by the Arminian police authorities towards prisoners suspected of anarchistic tendencies, I was compelled to devise some means of escaping the vigilance of the secret police agents who would be sure to infest the railway stations with a full description of my personality in their pockets.

The plan I eventually hit upon was a very simple one. Instead of proceeding to Wittichau, where I might have been seized, I passed the night in walking a distance of some twenty miles to the next railroad town. Here, after due inquiry, I boarded a train bound for a southern junction, where I changed for Berolingen, thereby returning to the capital by a roundabout route which no one, coming from Wittichau, would be expected to take. To make assurance doubly sure, I left the train a couple of stations before the terminus, and rode into the city on one of the numerous car lines that connect it with the surrounding places.

The detour I made cost me a delay of more than six hours, and it was towards eight o'clock the next evening when I at last reached my lodgings in the Kanonierstrasse. I was weary and disgusted—

disgusted at being footballed about in this humiliating fashion from one puzzling situation to the other, and more than ever determined to turn my back upon a country where my experiences had all been of so fruitless and disappointing a nature.

Had I only carried this determination into effect there and then, I should have been spared much subsequent pain and regret. But, as if everything conspired to urge me further along on the career I had once launched upon, an incident now occurred which overthrew all my fine resolves and revived in me once more in all its vigour that luckless spirit of adventure which recent events had all but quelled. It was this.

Upon my arrival at my lodgings, my landlady, a good-natured old soul, who in the palmy days of her youth had been an actress of some repute at the Court of St. Petersburg, drew my attention to an oblong box, some three feet long, which had been left at my address on the previous day. I had paid no heed to the matter at first, being engrossed with other thoughts; but the persistent anxiety of the good old lady that I should open the box and examine its contents led me to suspect that she had given way to her curiosity during my absence, and already knew what it contained. To humour her whim, therefore, I proceeded to open the thing, when, to my astonishment, I found neatly packed up in it the complete costume of an English courtier of the fifteenth century, together with a sword and a mask. Pinned to the packet was a large gilt-edged official card, issued from the Imperial. Chamberlain's office and inviting the attendance of Mr. Walter Raleigh, late Stallmeister to her Highness the Dowager Duchess of Bieberstein, at the masked ball given that night by their Majesties the Emperor and the Empress of Arminia in celebration of the fifth anniversary of their wedding.

I stood completely confused. The thought of the court ball had gone clean out of my head. Even the sight of the many carriages driving through the streets, with gorgeously-dressed cavaliers and ladies inside, which I had met on my way through the city that evening, had not recalled the fact to my mind. Doubtless, I reflected, as I now remembered the note I had received just before my dismissal from the ducal household of Bieberstein, Herr von Retzow had sent me these things before leaving Berolingen, little dreaming that by the time I used them the relations existing between us would have become the reverse of friendly.

I say "by the time I used them," for I will not pretend that I wavered for one instant as to what I should do under the circumstances. The temptation to plunge once more into the mysterious life I was just about to quit was simply irresistible in the form it presented itself to me, and I made no idle feint of withstanding it.

Glancing at my watch, I saw that it was barely a quarter to nine. The ball was not likely to commence before ten. I had ample time, therefore, to don my toggery, drive to the palace, and present myself boldly for admittance. What I should do when I arrived there was a matter to which I gave no thought. I left it simply to chance or the happy inspiration of the moment. The one all-important thing to me was that the man whose dupe I felt I had been for so long had unwittingly placed in my hands a weapon which could be used against him, and I was determined to avail myself of it to the very fullest extent.

I wasted no time in useless reflections, but, gently forcing my garrulous old landlady to leave my room, quickly exchanged my dusty, travel-stained clothes for the finery now spread out before me, and within less than an hour of my return home was well on my way to the Imperial palace.

THE INCIDENT OF THE WIFE'S
DOUBLE AND THE TRAGEDY
AT THE MASKED BALL

THE masked ball given in commemoration of the wedding of their Majesties the present Emperor and Empress of Arminia is, I am told, the first and, so far, the only instance of its kind recorded in the history of European court festivities. But the Emperor Willibald II. is nothing if not original. He loves to surprise the world with unusual spectacles, and it is but just to say that his success in this direction has been complete.

I am not going to attempt a description of the brilliant spectacular scene that unfolded itself before my eyes that night. It would require a far more facile pen than mine to accomplish such a task. To me its effect was simply bewildering, and I moved about for the first hour like one in a dream, seeking in vain to awaken to a clear sense of my surroundings. I had come there with the vague notion that, once admitted to the precincts of the Imperial palace, it would be comparatively easy to gain the car of the sovereign himself. But I soon found that all approach to the apartments reserved for the Imperial circle was strictly barred to the ordinary guests, among whom I numbered.

As I made my way through the gay and motley throng that crowded the vast apartments, I was accosted, at intervals, some half a dozen times by various masks, both male and female, but the remarks they addressed to me consisted only of the ordinary banter common between masqueraders all the world over. The speakers were all unknown to me, and I am certain that they were unaware of the identity of the person they were addressing.

At length, wearying of this aimless wandering from place to place, and tired of being buffeted and jostled about by the eager crowd in the great state rooms, I sought the quieter atmosphere of one of the smaller apartments adjoining the winter garden, where I retired to a secluded corner and proceeded to revolve the situation in my mind. It seemed folly to have come here and to leave again without having even attempted to gain the Emperor's ear. Supposing I boldly approached the Imperial circle and demanded access to His Majesty on urgent business? Probably I should be regarded as a madman and promptly removed, thereby losing all chance of ever effecting my purpose. I thought of conveying my warning by means of a written message. But who would undertake to place it in the Emperor's hands? In short, I devised half a dozen different plans, only to cast them aside again as impracticable, until I grew disheartened and rose impatiently, uttering an imprecation upon all princes and potentates and the foolish restrictions with which they hedge themselves in.

In my impulsiveness I must have spoken aloud, for two masks who happened to pass by at that moment turned round and glanced across at me. It may have been my fancy, but I certainly thought I saw one of them start slightly, as if struck by something in my appearance, and I drew back into the corner I had just quitted to avoid their attention.

They passed on, however, and, forgetting the incident, I relapsed into my reverie, from which I was presently again awakened by a light touch on my shoulder. Looking up, I saw standing before me the mask I had noticed a few moments ago. He wore the ancient costume of a court jester, with cap and bells, and, concluding from his appearance that he was about to perpetrate some piece of foolery, which I was not in the mood just then to receive graciously, I remained sitting in a posture indicative of extreme indifference.

The first words he uttered, however, dispelled all such notion and caused me to alter my attitude instantly.

"So pensive, valiant knight?" he said. "Surely, when so many bright eyes are shining, it looks ill for such a *preux chevalier* to sit sulking in a solitary corner."

The short, decisive tone sounded only too familiar to me, and I felt my heart beat faster. Dared I believe that the opportunity I had sought so long was here within my grasp, at the very moment when I had renounced all hope of ever securing it? I rose quickly and gazed searchingly at the speaker.

"Appearances are sometimes deceptive," I replied, without making any attempt to disguise my voice, though this would have been needless, for my accent must have betrayed me. "It is not always the costume that proclaims the man, wise mask."

"True," he rejoined, with a short laugh. "As an instance in point, we have the fable of the ass in the lion's skin."

"I have even met with instances," I said, fixing a meaning look upon his costume, "where the case of the fable was reversed, which happens when the lion poses in the ass's skin."

"Spoken like a true courtier," the mask replied, with a touch of irony, "which proves that the costume sometimes alters, if it does not make, the man. Since your vocation as a protector of high-born dames has proved so signal a failure, Mr. Stallmeister, it is, perhaps, wise of you to seek fortune in other fields, and a courtier's life is not amiss—when the sun shines."

"I fear I am past learning the craft," I said boldly, for I knew now to whom I was speaking. "And yet," I added in a lower tone, "I am able at this moment to render the Emperor of Arminia a service which he would ask in vain of the most devoted of his courtiers."

"What," he exclaimed mockingly, "have we discovered the lost Princess of Bieberstein?"

"The Princess of Bieberstein," I answered promptly, nettled by his taunting tone, "is at present at Wittichau in Silesia, where those who look may find her."

"Your information is somewhat faulty, my gallant knight," he rejoined quietly. "The Princess is at present within these very walls, or my knowledge of petticoats and their wearers is poorer than I think it."

This staggered me a little, and I was puzzled to find a suitable reply.

"Notwithstanding," I said at last, recovering my assurance, "I can assert most positively that it is scarcely four-and-twenty hours since I met Her Highness face to face in Wittichau, where," I added, lowering my voice once more, "I also learned other news that deeply concerns his Majesty the Emperor."

I thought I saw the keen grey eyes beneath the mask fix themselves sharply upon my face.

"There is an Arminian proverb," he remarked coldly, "that says, 'his tune I pipe whose bread I eat.' What reason has the Emperor to trust news coming from such a quarter?"

"There is some news that speaks for the sincerity of its bearer," I replied, understanding the implied accusation. "If I had the good fortune to gain his Majesty's ear, I would begin by warning him to beware of Heinrich von Retzow."

There was a pause before he answered, and I felt the glance of the eyes that rested upon me grow deeper and more searching.

"May be the Emperor has larger birds to secure than Heinrich von Retzow," he said. "Let those, however, who keep his company take care that the net, when it closes over him, does not include them. But what of this news? My time is brief."

He had fallen into the quick, imperative manner of speech which I remembered so well from my first meeting with him on the Square fronting the Arch of Victory. I had thought it so simple to convey my story to his ears. But, confronted as I now found myself with the actual task, I felt unutterably confused and embarrassed. To tell even an ordinary being that a scheme is on foot to have him judged insane and deprived of power and liberty is a ticklish undertaking at the best, but when that being happens to be an Emperor, and a quick-tempered one to boot, the matter is calculated to tax a cooler head than mine. Nor do I know exactly to this day how I accomplished the thing. All I can recollect is stammering more or less confused and incoherent answers to a series of quick, imperious questions, and experiencing a feeling something akin to that of a school-boy rehearsing a lesson to a master whose knowledge of the subject is already perfect.

He must have questioned me with a sort of instinct, for, confused though I was, I am certain that I omitted no detail of any importance, from the exact tenor of the conversation I had overheard in the garden of the hostelry at Wittichau to the meeting between the "Doctor" and Herr von Retzow in the passage of the house. And he listened to it all calmly and critically, like a general receiving the report of one of his scouts, without word or gesture denoting either surprise or any other emotion. Only when I had concluded, which I did with a recital of my flight through the inn window, and my hairbreadth escape from the bullets sent after me by Herr von Retzow, I thought I saw a twinkle of amused interest gleam in the eyes behind the mask.

"You have had a narrow escape," he said. "Let it be a warning to you not to mix with company you do not know. And now," he added sternly, "not a word of what you have heard to living soul. It is but one link more in the long chain of crime and treason that has been forging for months, and they little know, the fools, that there is one on their trail who will snap it in twain like a thread of rotten silk."

He spoke the last words in a tone of grim contentment, rather to himself than to me, and I think for the moment he forgot that I was there to overhear them.

"It would be well," I ventured to remark, somewhat audaciously, "not to delay the final blow too long, or it may fall when it is too late."

He looked at me gravely.

"He who strikes slowly strikes surely," he answered, to my surprise nowise offended. "But no more of this. Hush!" and he drew me back into the niche where I had been sitting, just as a mask costumed as a Turk entered the apartment to our left, and, after looking cautiously around and behind him, glided swiftly through the room and out at the opposite door.

"If you would render me a service," my companion whispered quickly, "follow that mask, and bring me word who it is. Stay, you will not meet me again. If you are successful, write your message on a slip of paper, and hand it to the officer of the palace guard, with the words, 'For the king's jester,' and it will reach me."

With these words he was gone, and I hastened away to execute my mission. The room seemed to be whirling round with me, so great was my excitement; for now, I thought, I was at last on the eve of the realisation of my dream. Had I only had the presence of mind to warn the Emperor against one whom I believed to be a still greater traitor than Herr von Retzow himself, and the more dangerous, too, inasmuch as he enjoyed his Majesty's full confidence. I mean Colonel Heinrich von Stauffenberg, over whose house at the Thiergarten the arch-plotter Von Retzow apparently exercised complete mastership. But it was too late to remedy the omission now, and I had to trust to good fortune for a renewal of the opportunity I had lost.

As I passed quickly into the next apartment in pursuit of the Turk, fully determined to gain a view of his features, even if I should have to tear his mask off by brute force, a difficulty presented itself to my mind which, in my eagerness, I had not thought of. How was I to identify the man when I did see him? There were probably not half a dozen people among the fifteen hundred guests assembled there with whose faces and personal appearance I was acquainted, excepting the members of the Imperial house, who were, of course, more or less familiar to me.

Still, I was resolved not to be at a loss to overcome so trifling an obstacle. If matters came to a pinch, I thought to myself, there was always the possibility of picking a quarrel with the man, in which event an immediate exchange of names, as a preliminary to further action, would become necessary according to the Arminian code of honour.

I had not followed my friend the Turk for more than a few seconds, however, when I became aware that I was not alone in my pursuit of him. A female mask, clad as a wood nymph, was always close at his heels, following him from room to room, and evidently bent on gaining speech with him. Soon I perceived that it was she whom he was endeavouring to evade, and I felt curious to watch the progress of the strange little comedy.

For some time he continued on his quick course from apartment to apartment, threading his way always purposely through the throng where it was thickest, no doubt hoping thereby to escape the attentions of his pursuer. But the attempt was vain, for she stuck to her task with a persistency that was little short of admirable. Presently, with a gesture of impatience, he turned about and faced his fair tormentor. In an instant she was at his side and whispered something in his ear which I was not near enough to hear. He started like a guilty man, recovered himself quickly, and answered evidently with some masquerade pleasantry. But the nymph was not to be put off. They were now in the gallery of sculptures, to which opened a series of small chambers, each filled with a special class of art treasures, and, placing her arm in his, she motioned with her head significantly towards one of the doors, indicating that she wished to be conducted there.

No cavalier could have refused such an appeal on the part of a lady; and the Turk, seeing himself fairly caught at last, submitted with as good a grace as he could summon. The moment they had passed through the doorway I slipped noiselessly behind the huge drapery which half covered the entrance, and, concealing myself behind its folds, quietly awaited the development of events.

"You talk in riddles, fair nymph," I heard the Turk say. "I know no such person as you name."

"Why persist in keeping up this make-believe, Ernest?" the nymph answered in a low monotonous voice. "We are alone. If I dared, I would remove my mask, to prove I am she whom you have wronged. By the memory of——"

She lowered her voice at this point to so faint a whisper that I could not catch the words. But their effect upon the Turk was startling.

"Anna, great heavens!" he exclaimed, clutching her arm, "are you mad? Do you know what you have risked by venturing here?"

"What have I left to risk?" she replied, with a slight tremor in her voice. "Have you not taken from me all that makes a woman's life worth living? My trust, and my faith, and my hope? These you cannot restore to me, for they are gone for ever. But my honour, too, is in your possession, and you shall return it to me, or answer for it before a tribunal which recognises no distinction between man and man."

"This is folly, Anna," the other replied. "What I have done I have done to save you from the consequences of your own blind passion, for you would have delivered our secret into hands that would have used it ruthlessly against us both. I have foes that you know not of, child," he continued; "wretched, bloodthirsty vampires, who fatten upon a court scandal like vultures upon a carcass. Think of it calmly, Anna; where on God's earth should a wife's honour be safe if not in her husband's keeping?"

"In her husband's?" the nymph echoed scornfully. "Who is to prove that I have a husband? Or that you are my husband? The page on which our marriage was recorded has been removed from the register."

"Not at my doing, nor with my knowledge or consent," he said quickly. "I swear it."

"But you have robbed me of my proof," the nymph retorted. "The certificate—where is it?"

"In my keeping," he answered, almost sternly, "where it shall remain. Foolish girl, why this persistent distrust of my love and my honour? That paper would be worthless but for the love that makes it binding upon me before man as before God. If I cared—but, for Heaven's sake, let us end this tragical talk. I am not suited for it. Let us be friends, Anna, and trust each other. If I am not a saint—and I have never made pretence to the title—I am, at least, not the devil they paint me."

I think he must have approached her with some tender gesture, for I heard a rustling of garments, as if she were retreating from him; and the next moment the question came in the same low, toneless voice as before—

"How can I believe that you love me still, when all the world knows you are courting another?"

"You will listen to no reason, Anna," he replied. "Have I not told you that policy compels me to make this feint of obeying the Emperor's commands?"

"But the Princess of Bieberstein? What of her?"

"I care no more for the Princess of Bieberstein," he exclaimed, "than for any other living woman, yourself excepted, Anna."

"Yet you are even now wooing her," she persisted, "and she who is wooed may be won. What then?"

"There is no danger," he answered curtly.

"How can you tell? She is a woman, and where one woman loves, why may not another?"

"Anna," he said impatiently, "can I do more than swear to you that the Princess will never take your place in my heart?"

"Then you are deceiving her."

"If you choose to call it by that name," he said in a tone of indifference.

"How can I choose to call it otherwise?" she answered slowly. "She may return your feigned love with true."

"She will not."

"But she may. What then?"

"It is her affair," he answered almost brutally. "What care I?"

There was a sound like the drawing of a deep breath, followed by so long a pause that I thought the strange couple had moved away. Then, suddenly, came another sound, quick and startling, resembling something between the snap of a gun that has missed fire, and the noise made by the violently clapping to of a book. It was so peculiarly suggestive that I involuntarily drew aside the drapery behind which I was concealed and peeped forth into the room.

The scene I saw there was strange indeed. The nymph had vanished, and in the middle of the room, his countenance comically expressive of rueful surprise, stood Duke Ernest Frederick of Friedrichsburg. At his feet lay his mask, the fastening torn asunder, while on his left cheek the imprint left by five small fingers showed with painful distinctness.

The whole thing passed my understanding, for, in truth, anything more unexpected than this abrupt and violent ending of the interview I had overheard could scarcely be conceived. As for the Duke himself, I think his astonishment must have deprived him temporarily of the power of movement, for he stood for a while in the posture I have described like one paralysed, staring into vacancy as if a ghost had just appeared to him. Presently the spell passed. He stooped, picked up his mask, and darted towards the door, where I had now stepped out and confronted him.

"Out of the way, fool!" he exclaimed, endeavouring to push me aside, and at the same time holding his mask before his face. "I have no time for pleasantries."

But I gripped him by the arm and detained him.

"I crave but a few moments' interview, Duke Ernest of Friedrichsburg," I said; "and I promise your Highness that our talk shall touch upon no pleasantry."

He started at hearing his name.

"You have mistaken your man," he said. "Stand aside, and let me pass."

"Not until you have listened to me," I answered, maintaining my hold upon him. "It may be mere diplomacy to deny yourself to a woman. To do so to a man savours of cowardice."

His attitude altered instantly. He shook himself free from my grasp, and raised his hand as if to strike me.

"You dare——" he began in a voice of passion. But he checked himself with an effort. "Who are you?" he asked abruptly; "and by what right do you dare to address me thus?"

I removed my mask.

"My name is Walter Raleigh," I answered. "Perhaps it is not so well known to your Highness as my face."

He stared at me for a moment with a puzzled expression. Evidently he was struggling to find a place for me in his memory.

"It may help to refresh your Highness's memory," I continued, "if I refer back to a certain night at a certain house in the Waldstrasse, and to a certain incident that occurred thereafter, in which the crown of my head played one part, and I believe your Highness's sword the other. I am not accustomed to accept blows without paying for them, and I am here to liquidate my indebtedness."

He recognised me now.

"Has the madhouse been let loose tonight?" he exclaimed. "How am I to understand this strange introduction?"

"As your Highness pleases," I answered. "I am merely curious to ascertain whether your Highness's sword is as effective when used in front of an adversary as it is when used at his back."

He had lowered the hand in which he held his mask, and stood regarding me with a look that would be difficult to describe. All I noted—and I noted it with inner contentment—was the rising anger that flashed in his fine dark eyes and played in ominous twitchings round the corners of his mouth.

"To put it plainly," he said, speaking with forced coldness, "you mean to demand satisfaction at my hands for some imaginary grievance or insult?"

"Scarcely imaginary," I said, "unless your Highness pleases to assert that the blow I received two months ago was dealt by another hand than yours; in which case," I added, "I should merely alter the grounds of my challenge. I have a rich choice to offer your Highness."

"For instance?" he said. I think he began to be amused at my persistency.

"For instance," I replied, "the betrayal of the woman whom I once had the honour to love, and who has no friend to champion her rights save myself. But perhaps your Highness does not find it convenient to recollect that such a person exists as the Countess of Lausitz."

A dark flush spread over his features at these words, and he advanced towards me threateningly.

"Fellow!" he said passionately, "you shall rue this insolence."

"That is as it may be," I retorted. "I am here, prepared to answer for myself at the sword's point."

"Pooh, you are a madman," he said. "One does not tight within the walls of a palace."

"There is the palace garden," I suggested.

"Nor with a man one doesn't know," he continued, ignoring the hint.

"That I am here is evidence that I possess the rights and privileges of gentle blood," I said.

"I prefer to trust the evidence of my own eyes, which proclaims you a desperate adventurer, if not something worse," he replied.

"It is probably the more prudent conclusion for one who values his skin more than his honour," I remarked.

"By God!" he exclaimed; "I am tempted to give you a lesson that will teach you to curb that scurrilous tongue of yours."

"If by that your Highness means that you are tempted to fight," I said, "I may observe that I have never met a man who was more difficult to tempt."

This clinched it. I saw the hot blood rush once more to his face, and his hand went instinctively to the hilt of his sword.

"I will meet you," he said; "but not now."

"It must be to-night," I said, "for my time hereafter may not be my own."

"In half an hour, then, at the great fountain in the palace garden."

"I shall be there, and await your Highness," I replied.

"You will bring your second?" he queried.

"Your Highness is aware," I answered, "that I can find no one to second me in a duel with the Duke of Friedrichsburg. We must fight without seconds or not at all."

"But this is somewhat out of the ordinary," he said, hesitating.

"If I can risk the consequences," I replied, "and I am willing, surely your Highness need have no fears."

"Let it be so, then," he said, after a moment's deliberation. "And the weapons?"

"I leave the choice to your Highness," I said.

"Swords, then?"

"Swords," I said. "But I must depend upon your Highness to procure them."

He bowed stiffly, turned away, stopped, and came back again.

"You are a gentleman, I am to presume," he said. "Will you pledge me your word that you will not betray my presence here to a living soul?"

The question startled me. I had forgotten all about my mission and the Emperor's desire to ascertain the identity of the masked Turk. Under the circumstances, it would, of course, be impossible to gratify his Majesty's curiosity.

"Your Highness need be under no apprehension on that score," I said. "I would warn you, however, to avoid a certain mask in the costume of a court jester, who is particularly anxious to obtain a view of your features."

"Ha," he exclaimed with a start, "that is the Emperor's costume. Have you seen him?"

"It is at his Majesty's commands," I replied, "that I have been following and watching your Highness for the last half hour."

He gave me a perplexed look.

"You?" he said. "Upon my word, you seem to be playing a strange variety of parts here."

"It is from necessity, not from choice," I replied.

"At the fountain, then," he said abruptly, and, turning on his heel, he left me.

I could have shouted for joy. The possibility that my presence at the masked ball would afford me this opportunity to secure an encounter with the man against whom I felt so deep a resentment had never occurred to me for an instant. I had heard of the Duke as a reckless hothead, and had laid my lines accordingly. The complete success of my taunting challenge caused me a feeling of unspeakable elation.

Has the reader ever experienced that curious sensation which is produced by the magnetic power of a pair of human eyes directing their gaze upon him with intense earnestness from some unseen quarter? That sensation overcame me now with a suddenness that sent a shock through me, and I turned with the instinctive conviction that someone was watching me. Behind me was the doorway through which I had entered the room, and for the flash of an instant, as I turned, I fancied I saw two black eyes gleam out at me from the folds of the drapery overhanging it. This may have been a freak of my own imagination; but what could not be imagination was the sudden, unmistakable movement of the drapery itself, proving beyond a doubt that someone was concealed behind it, as I had concealed myself there some minutes before.

Striding quickly towards it, I pulled the folds of the drapery apart. No one was there. I passed out into the gallery beyond, and swept its whole length with my eyes in both directions, but I discovered no one to whom my suspicion could attach. There were a few groups scattered about at various points of the gallery, and here and there a solitary mask was passing leisurely along, or standing idly in contemplation of some specimen of the art treasures with which the place abounded. But the nearest of these was distant enough from where I stood to preclude the possibility of his or her being the person who had hidden behind the drapery.

Considerably perplexed, and not a little disturbed in my mind, I left the gallery, and, making my way downstairs, rejoined the throng in the great hall below. I had not mingled with the jostling crowd there above a minute or two, when I felt my sleeve pulled from behind, and, facing round, confronted a mask in the dress of a Swiss peasant girl.

"Quick, bend down and give me your ear," she whispered hurriedly. "I have something important to tell you."

I obeyed mechanically, and she continued, bringing her lips so close to my ear that I almost felt the touch of her mask against my cheeks—

"If you value your safety, leave the palace instantly. Linger another five minutes, and escape will be impossible."

I gave a light laugh, and looked keenly at the speaker, endeavouring, but in vain, to recognise the features beneath the covering of her black mask. All I saw was a pair of dark gleaming eyes fixed with a gaze half anxious, half threatening, upon mine.

"I wish," I said, speaking in as low a tone as she had, in order to disguise my voice the better, "that I were deserving of the interest you bestow upon me, fair mask. But I fear I cannot claim to be the person you think you are addressing."

"Fool!" she answered. "Other eyes, besides mine, have seen Walter Raleigh's face this evening, and know what disguise he wears. Remember Wittichau, and heed my warning. It is that of a friend."

With these startling words she was gone, before I had recovered sufficient presence of mind to think of detaining her. What could it mean? Who was my fair warner? There were but two women I knew of who could possess any knowledge of the recent events at Wittichau, and of these two I had but just identified the one, with my ears, if not with my eyes, during her animated converse with her husband, the Duke of Friedrichsburg.

Could this, then, have been the Princess of Bieberstein? I scouted the idea at once for various reasons. Though the size, the figure, and the general appearance might have corresponded, the movements, the gestures, and the manner of speech were entirely different. I elbowed my way as deftly as I could through the crowded room in the direction the mask had taken, determined to speak with her again and ascertain, if not who she was, at least the nature of the danger against which she had cautioned me. Nor had I proceeded above a few steps when I caught sight of her standing beneath a huge vase of Sèvres porcelain that filled the embrasure of one of the windows. Her eyes were fixed upon me with a watchful gaze, and it seemed to me that she had been awaiting my approach. If so, it was only to elude me, for she moved swiftly away before I had time to reach her, and a momentor two later she was watching me again from some other distant coign of vantage.

In this fashion she led me like some fantastic will-o'-the-wisp to and fro through some half a dozen apartments, always managing cleverly to keep a crowded space between herself and me, and thus thwart all my attempts to approach her, until I grew tired of being tricked, and, recognising that to follow her under such circumstances was mere waste of time, gave up the pursuit, and returned to the spot from which I had started.

And now a strange thing happened. If heretofore the mask had led and I had followed, there was now a reversal of the order of things, for, wherever I went, there I was sure to see, watching me with an eager glance from some remote corner of the room, the mask in the Swiss peasant's dress whom I had so vainly pursued some moments before. Evidently, for reasons best known to herself, she was following my movements, though whether to assure herself that I would obey her warning and leave the palace, or for some other purpose, it was impossible to guess. It flashed across me that she might be the person who had been concealed behind the drapery in the art gallery, and that, having overheard my conversation there with the Duke of Friedrichsburg, her warning to me and the subsequent dance she had led me were mere manæuvres to induce me to forego the meeting I had arranged with his Highness.

Imbued with this idea, I set about me to devise some means of ridding myself of her—a matter of comparative ease when once determined upon—and, leading her rapidly through a maze of halls and passage-ways, of the direction of which I was myself totally ignorant, I managed at last to give her the slip, as the slang phrase has it, among the crowd of dancers in the ball-room. Thence I proceeded with all possible speed to the famous winter garden, and, passing out on to the terrace, gained the garden below unhindered.

It wanted still five minutes to the hour appointed for the meeting, and I spent them in walking to and fro under the trees in the neighbourhood of the great fountain. The place was quite deserted, for it was a bleak night, though early in May, and, save for the fitful light that fell upon the garden in weird, fantastic streaks from the illuminated windows of the palace, all was dark and dreary there.

Would he come, after all? I thought to myself, as minute after minute slowly passed; and if so, would he come alone? A duel without seconds was a bold thing to undertake, even for a duke and the brother-in-law of an emperor, and I had wondered a little at his ready acquiescence in this necessary feature of our contemplated meeting. For myself, I had no fear of its consequences; but then I had laid my plans accordingly, and entertained no doubt as to what the ultimate outcome would be.

A brisk footstep upon the gravel aroused me from my thoughts. The next instant a dark figure emerged into the spray of light that played about the fountain, and looked searchingly around. It was the Duke.

I stepped forward and saluted him.

"Let us get to business quickly," he said, producing a pair of duelling swords from beneath his mantle. He was still dressed as a Turk, but he had divested himself of certain upper parts of the costume, which would have been likely to embarrass his movements.

He presented the weapons to me for my choice, holding them by the blade. I drew one, and we measured lengths. He then drew a note-book from his pocket, tore out two leaves, upon one of which he wrote something, and handed it to me together with the blank leaf.

"It is a formality which it is desirable in both our interests to observe under these somewhat extraordinary circumstances," he said.

I read what he had written. It was as follows:—

"I, Duke Ernest Frederick of Friedrichsburg, being about to fight a duel without seconds with Mr. Walter Raleigh, hereby declare that, whatever the issue of said duel may be, it is to be regarded strictly as a contest of honour and judged accordingly."

Below his signature he had added the date and the precise hour of our meeting.

I understood. Bowing, I took the pencil he proffered me and wrote upon the blank leaf a declaration in identical terms, merely reversing the order of the names. This I handed back to him, and, retaining the other, stowed it away in my doublet. I could not help admiring the coolness and forethought of the man. Of his reputation as a swordsman I knew nothing whatever, but he was evidently well versed in the formalities attendant upon an encounter such as ours, and set about then execution with the keen relish of a schoolboy planning some forbidden frolic. He seemed to welcome the opportunity, probably rare to one of his birth and rank, of experiencing something of the reality of a soldier's life. And I liked him the better for it.

We now took our places, crossed blades, and the play began.

I say the play, for, at the risk of appearing a braggart, I must say that from the outset it was mere play to me. The Duke was fairly well schooled, and might have passed muster in the fencing room. But a good fencer and a good fighter are two very different things. It is like the learning of a foreign language at home. One may master it to perfection by the book, but, when it comes to the actual practical application, the best of scholars, with all his grammar and learning, figures but as a poor dunce until the practice and experience of everyday conversation come to his aid and teach him how to utilise his knowledge.

The coolness, the nerve, the deliberation—in short, everything apart from actual skill—that constitute the experienced swordsman were lacking in Duke Ernest. He fought excitedly, without plan or method, and with a nervous uncertainty that would have rendered him an easy victim to a far less skilled opponent than myself. Indeed, within the first thirty seconds, had I thought fit to end the contest, I could have done so with probably fatal consequences to his Highness. But I had other plans, and I continued to maintain the purely defensive attitude I had assumed from the beginning.

He saw that I was playing with him, and, to do him justice, the knowledge only stirred him to greater efforts. I fancy he thought my purpose was to tire him out, and then, throwing aside my reserve, to assume the offensive. But my intentions were quite different. I proposed to humiliate him, not to shed his blood, and I was merely awaiting my opportunity to execute a certain trick which one may occasionally see performed by fencing-masters, and which consists in neatly disarming your opponent at the very moment when a false parry leads him to believe you are at his mercy. It is a pretty device, but dangerous to attempt, for the slightest miscarriage in an actual combat means certain defeat, if not death itself.

Alas, that I waited as long as I did. But it was not until my ear caught the ominous sound of someone moving near the fountain that I seriously prepared for the final *coup*. Then, seized with the fear that I might be baulked at the last moment of the empty triumph I had foolishly set my heart upon securing, I quickly changed my tactics, and passing from the attitude of defence, which I had until then assumed, to one of vigorous attack, I began to press my man close and hard.

The opportunity I had been looking for came almost instantly. With a sharp, whizzing sound the Duke's weapon flew into the air, and then—— How it occurred, God knows. All I saw, at the very instant when my own weapon shot forward, was some dark object suddenly interposed between myself and the Duke. In vain I endeavoured to alter the direction of my blade. It was too late. There was a shriek and a low, moaning cry, and slowly the figure between us glided to the ground.

It must have been several seconds before either of us could stir. Then we both knelt down beside the prostrate form upon the grass and gazed upon it in a helpless, aimless fashion.

"Great Heaven!" I murmured, "it is the Swiss peasant girl."

The Duke clutched my arm convulsively.

"Remove her mask," he said in a hoarse whisper. "Quick, man, I must see her face."

Did he know? Had he guessed? The horror of the thing is still upon me as I write. I did as he bade me, and knelt there staring at the uplifted face like one transfixed. The features I had disclosed were those of his own wife.

With a great cry of agony he threw himself upon the lifeless body.

"Anna, my own!" he cried; "speak to me, my sweet. It is I, your husband. Speak to me, dear, speak!"

His voice died away in a stifled sob. Alas! she would never speak to him again, for my blade had passed through her heart, and she was dead. He rose to his feet with a wild, frantic gesture.

"It is my wife," he said in a hollow tone, gripping me with both his hands and shaking me. "Do you understand, man? It is my wife, and she is dead. What is to be done?"

But I was too dazed to reply, and I still knelt there motionless, staring at the dead face upon the grass as if it were an apparition from another world. Was it all some devil's play of my own fancy? If this was the wife of Duke Ernest, the girl that had so cruelly jilted me, who, then, was the wood nymph whose conversation with the Duke I had overheard that night? Dulled as my senses were by the frightful occurrence, it was only gradually that the whole obvious truth broke in upon them, and I recognised what a blind fool I had been. Nay, worse almost than blind, not even to have seen through so palpable a trick as that played upon Duke Ernest that night, when, in the belief that he was conversing with his wife, he had been duped into confirming the story of his marriage to the Princess of Bieberstein herself. The disappearance of the Princess, her journey to Wittichau, and her subsequent reappearance with her ill-fated companion at the masked ball—it was all explained to me now.

What a hideous mingling of farce and tragedy, I thought, as I gazed stupidly at the Duke, who had thrown himself once more beside the fair corpse. It seemed like a weird dream, a dread, overwhelming nightmare. I felt a thousand things, and could give utterance to but one.

"I have killed her," I murmured at last in a dull, disconsolate fashion, "and must abide the consequences. I will go for assistance."

He sprang to his feet and held me back.

"Fool!" he exclaimed hotly. "Would you place a baiter round your neck? You must fly."

I stared at him.

"I have killed her," I repeated vacantly, "and will abide the consequences."

There was a confused sound of voices in the distance, and a number of lights could be seen whisking about below the terrace of the palace. Evidently the alarm had been given by someone, and people wore approaching the spot where we stood. Duke Ernest seized me by the shoulder and pushed me away.

"Go," he said, "and leave all explanations to me. You are lost if you stay."

I still hesitated, and he burst into a fit of fury.

"By the God that is above us!" he exclaimed, picking up the sword from the grass, "I will run you through the body if you do not obey me. You have trifled with me already beyond endurance. Do you think, because you are the better swordsman, that I am not a man, with a man's sense of right and honour? Go, I say. She died, thinking to save me. It was her fault, not yours. I can explain. You cannot."

I turned mechanically to go.

"Not that way," he exclaimed. "Take the path that passes to the left by the lower terrace. It will bring you to a gate leading to the public Square. Lift the inner latch, and pass out."

He had a clearer head than I at this critical moment, and I went like a schoolboy obeying his master's behest. When I caught the last glimpse of him, as I turned and looked back before rounding a cluster of trees that cut him off from my view, he stood resting upon the sword he had picked up a moment before. His gaze was fixed downwards upon the lifeless form stretched out at his feet, but I could not see his features, and was left to imagine their expression.

Through the trees I now saw three men with lanterns hurrying towards him. They were palace servants, and I hastened on to escape them. I reached the gate unnoticed, and passed out into the Square. The place was alive with conveyances of every description. I hailed a droschky, jumped in, and ordered the man to drive me home.

What I should do when I got there, or what I should do thereafter, were questions that did not enter my thoughts then. I had a murder on my conscience—a murder of which I was innocent, and yet guilty—and as I drove along I saw nothing, and knew of nothing, but the dead face of the girl I had loved peering at me out of the darkness that surrounded me.

THE INCIDENT OF THE ARREST OF WALTER RALEIGH AND THE MAN WITH THE MISSING FOREFINGER

I MAY puss over the next four-and-twenty hours of my life in silence. The reader, I fancy, will not he particularly concerned to hear anything I could say regarding the effect produced upon my mind by the terrible calamity of which I had been the unwilling cause, nor could I hope to do anything like justice to the subject.

Suffice it to say that I was dominated by a feeling of total callousness as to what the future might bring me, and that, could I have undone what was done by sacrificing every hope and ambition that had ever stirred my soul, I would have willingly submitted to the sacrifice. I cannot say with certainty whether, during this earliest period of utter, crushing desolation, I was alive to any sense of the personal danger in which I stood. I know that upon the first occasion of my venturing again into the streets of Berolingen, which I did the day after the masked ball, I became conscious that my movements were being watched. But the circumstance excited no other feeling in me than one of contemptuous indifference. The idea of flight had never entered my head. The possibility of my being arrested and tried for murder or manslaughter may have occurred to me; but that is all. It excited no fear in my breast, for I would not have cared a snap of the fingers for the severest sentence any judge in Christendom could have passed upon me.

I had spent, so far as I can remember, two whole days and nights in this desperate frame of mind, waiting for a development of some sort or other, and earing but little what it might prove to be, when an occurrence befell that aroused my faculties once more from the state of lethargy into which they had lapsed and gave me food for much puzzled thought.

I have already stated that, after the tragedy in the palace garden, I found my footsteps dogged wherever I went. For what purpose, or at whose behest, I knew not nor cared to inquire. I dodged my pursuers and eluded their vigilance, not with any desire to escape from them, but merely for the pastime it afforded me. On one such occasion—it was the second night after the masked ball—when I had success-fully given my self-constituted body-guard the slip and was return-ing home to my lodgings by a circuitous route through a lonely part of the city, I was stopped by a couple of men, one of whom asked me the way to a certain spot in the neighbourhood. Something in the fellow's physiognomy put me on my guard, and instead of reply-ing I stepped quickly back—fortunately just in time to prevent the second one from attacking me in the rear. This latter ruffian had a knife in his hand, which I seized and wrenched from him before he could bring it into play, and the next moment I had landed a blow on his companion's chest which sent him reeling into the gutter. The promptness of the action evidently confounded the worthy couple, for the man whose knife I had appropriated fled instantly with great precipitation, whilst his mate, after picking himself up from the heap of refuse on to which he had fallen, followed with as much speed as he could command.

I proceeded on my way, a good deal exercised in my mind by this occurrence. That the attack had been a premeditated one there could be no doubt. I knew the faces of both the men, having met them, during the last two days, on more than one occasion, though without suspecting the existence of any connection between them and those who had been shadowing me. On reaching my lodgings I saw one of these latter posted in a doorway on the opposite side of the street, and, angered at the insolence of the thing, I crossed over and ap-proached him deliberately.

He did not stir, but awaited my coming as one would that of an old acquaintance, nodding a friendly greeting as I reached him.

"You scoundrel!" I said, measuring him from top to toe, "tell your employer, whoever he is, that it takes more than one arm, and more than one knife, to give the happy despatch to Walter Raleigh. As for this thing, you may return it to your vile accomplice, and let him know that if he comes within reach of this fist again he shall not escape as easily as he did to-night."

Saying which, I threw the knife at the fellow's feet, and turning my hack upon him walked across the street to my lodgings. The look of blank astonishment on his face, as the knife fell with a clanging sound on the pavement, was a perfect picture. But it was not until the next day that I comprehended its full meaning.

Taken by itself, I should not have thought this miserable attempt upon my life worth recording in these pages. But it was repeated the following day in so bold and determined a manner, and was this time accompanied by such strangely contradictory circumstances, that I could not pass it over without omitting a very peculiar link in the chain of events which I am presenting to the reader.

On this second occasion, though it happened in the full light of the noonday sun, when I was traversing the Siegesplatz, or Place of Victory, which fronts the Gate of Brandenburg, I did not gain a view of my assailant's face at all. All I became aware of was the peculiar shrieking noise of a bullet as it whizzed close by my left ear, followed by a stinging sensation in the lobe of that organ. There was no report—at least, I heard none—which proved that the weapon from which the bullet had been discharged was an air-gun, or some similar kind of devil's instrument. Glancing instinctively in the direction whence the shot must have been fired, I saw a man running at full speed between the trees of the Thiergarten, which skirts the square in the west.

Before I had time to determine in my own mind whether it would be worth while under the circumstances to attempt to capture the scoundrel, there being about two hundred yards between us, and he having the advantage of an easy escape into the thick of the forest, I saw that someone else had taken up the chase, and I stood still to await the result. This, however, was a foregone conclusion, for long before the pursuer, who must have been walking some fifty yards behind me, reached the outskirts of the wood, the fellow had disappeared altogether from view, and further pursuit became useless.

The whole thing had passed without attracting the slightest notice among the public in the square, and pressing my handkerchief to my ear to staunch the blood that was flowing from it, I now hurried across the place towards the spot where my would-be assassin had vanished. Judge of my astonishment when I came up with the man who had given chase to the fellow and recognised in him one of those who had been shadowing me for the last three days. It was, in fact, the very individual with whom I had spoken the night before on returning home after my tussle with the two villains in the street.

"You have been hit," he said, before I could address him. "You had better get your wound dressed at once."

"It is a mere scratch," I answered, "and requires no dressing. What is of more importance to me is to know who the villain is that fired at me."

"He is evidently no friend of yours," the man answered, with grim humour.

"So I presume," I said. "Perhaps he is one of yours."

The same surprised look came into the man's face that I had noticed in it the previous night, when I threw the assassin's knife at his feet.

"I cannot prevent you from thinking so," he replied, "but I know no more of the fellow than you do."

"Then why do you follow and watch me?" I asked.

"I obey my orders," he said.

"Orders? From whom?"

"That is my concern."

"Are you a police officer?"

In lieu of answering he merely shrugged his shoulders and smiled knowingly.

"I can scarcely suppose," I went on, "that you have been set at my heels to protect me from the attacks of these murderous villains."

"I have no instructions on that score," he answered. "It would be well, though," he went on, "if you walked rather less abroad than you do; and," he added confidentially, "if you will take a hint from me, you will change your lodgings. You have some determined enemies, and, if I am not much mistaken, they will effect their purpose yet, unless you take measures to elude them."

With this he gave me a nod that was intended to be encouraging, and left me standing. I was now scarcely much wiser than before, save that I knew, what I had not known previously, that I had two sets of shadowers to deal with, the object of one of which was to take my life, and that of the other God knows what.

It was by no means an enviable situation. Although my worst enemy cannot accuse me of being a coward, I must confess to having experienced a thrill of dismay at the prospect before me, and for the space of a moment or two I even meditated flight from the dangers surrounding me. But I discarded this latter idea at once. Berolingen just now possessed an attraction for me which, call it morbid or not, was far too powerful to be outweighed by considerations of personal safety. It is said that those whose hands are tainted with innocent blood are subject to a strange spell which forces them to hover near the scene where the deed of horror was committed. Perhaps I was under the influence of some such spell. At any rate, I felt irresistibly drawn to the vicinity of the Imperial palace, and spent hours and hours, both by night and by day, watching every outlet of the building in the expectation of seeing the remains of my erstwhile love borne out for burial.

At last I had a new channel into which to divert my thoughts. It was towards evening on the day of my adventure on the Siegesplatz, and I was packing up my belongings prior to quitting my lodgings—for I had decided, not unwisely, I think, to follow my strange adviser's counsel and quit my present quarters—when the following note was delivered into my hands by a street messenger—

"I shall expect you to-night at the usual time and place. If you value your safety, do not fail to come. H. v. R."

It was certainly short and to the point, but it surprised me beyond measure. Truth to say, engrossed as I had been with the one overwhelming memory of the event at the masked ball, I had scarcely given any further thought to Herr von Retzow and his double dealings. It had occurred to my mind once or twice that it was perhaps he upon whose instructions my life was being sought, but I was too indifferent as to the source of these desperate attempts to dwell at any length upon the subject. As for the possibility that I should ever again enter into personal intercourse with this man, I would have ridiculed the bare idea of such a thing.

Nevertheless, in spite of the cool presumption that characterised this message, and my strong suspicion that its writer was the real originator of the attacks upon my life, I decided without a moment's hesitation to comply with the summons. After all, I reflected, anything was preferable to the state of harassing uncertainty in which I was living, and though in venturing into the house at the Thiergarten I might be taking my life in my hands, I would at least go prepared not to part with it save at a heavy cost to those who should attempt to deprive me of it.

Having once formed this resolve, I felt my interest in things mundane revive again, and after passing the evening in hunting for some suitable quarters where I might hope to escape the unwelcome notice of my persecutors should I require such a hiding-place after that night, I repaired towards midnight to the well-known house near the Thiergarten.

The door was opened by the servant who had received Herr von Retzow and myself on the night when I first formed the famous police agent's acquaintance. Following a purpose of my own, I asked the man whether Colonel von Stauffenberg was within. He looked surprised at the question, but replied promptly that his Excellency was at Potshof, in attendance upon his Majesty. This I know to be true, for I had been in Potshof myself that very forenoon, and had seen the Colonel in the flesh driving with the Emperor in the Lustgarten. I would have questioned the man further, but, having answered my first inquiry, he cut my next one short by saying that, "the Herr Commissar awaited me," and inviting me with a polite gesture to follow him.

I had no other alternative but to comply, and a moment later I was ushered into the presence of Herr von Retzow. I slipped my hand into my hip pocket to assure myself that my revolver was handy, and then advanced into the room with an air of affected indifference. It was the same apartment in which I had partaken of his hospitality on the first occasion of my visiting the house, and I remembered its features well. There were three doors in the room, one by which I had entered, and one in each of the side walls. In the middle of the apartment stood a large square table, and near the window at the further end a small desk. At the latter sat Herr von Retzow himself, engaged with a heap of papers that were piled up in front of him.

He turned round in his chair as I entered and regarded me for a moment sharply.

"So you have come, after all, my dear Sir Walter," he said. "You have acted wisely."

There was not a trace of that harsh, forbidding accent in his voice which had repelled me so strongly when I last met him in Wittichau. Did he, I wondered, want to cajole me into keeping silent upon what I had seen and heard there?

"Doubtless," I said, "you have the best reasons for knowing that my coming would be uncertain. But, as you see, I am not so easily removed."

"Which means, I suppose, that you credit me with the intention of removing you," he answered coolly.

"If I needed proofs," I rejoined, "I should find little difficulty in producing them. I have not forgotten Wittichau."

He rose quietly from his seat, and looked me full in the face.

"Has it never occurred to you, my friend," he asked suavely, "that you made an unconscionable fool of yourself on that occasion?"

I believe I coloured like some raw schoolboy at the cool effrontery of the question. But, the devil knows, the man had a way of saying these things that took one's breath away.

"Maybe I did—from your point of view," I said. "But I am no abettor of treason and treachery, and I would have you know it."

"Bravely spoken, but none the less foolishly," he replied; "nor does it alter the fact, friend Sir Walter, that by your officious rashness on the occasion in question you narrowly missed spoiling the detective work of months."

"Ah!" I exclaimed, "would you have me believe—pooh! I am too old a bird to be caught by that kind of chaff. Was it excess of loyalty, pray, that caused you to send four bullets after me at Wittichau?"

I thought I had stumped him this time. But not a bit of it. He met my eye as frankly and fearlessly as ever.

"All things considered," he said deliberately, "I am not so sure that you deserved to escape as lightly as you did, for you sadly needed a lesson in discretion."

I laughed aloud. This attempt, as I thought it, to gloss over the shooting affair at Wittichau seemed to me too palpably lame.

"You mean to imply," I said, "that you missed your aim on purpose. A rather sorry excuse for poor marksmanship."

A flash as of angry scorn lighted up his eyes.

"You shall judge for yourself," he answered abruptly. "Come." He touched a hand-bell that stood upon his writing-desk, and the servant who had ushered me in entered.

"To the shooting gallery," he said; and before I knew what he meant, he had passed out of the door.

I followed him wonderingly, and a moment or two later found myself in a kind of outbuilding about forty feet in length, which evidently extended into the garden at the back of the house, and was fitted out as a miniature shooting range. As we entered, the servant who had preceded us touched an electric button, and the piece was instantly lighted up with the brightness of day. Upon a sign from my strange host, the man then placed a new target in position at the lower end. It was about two feet in diameter, and black, with a white bull's-eye. Pointing to a row of pistols arrayed ready for use on the shooting stand, Herr von Retzow said—

"The first shot shall be yours. Take your choice."

I shrugged my shoulders.

"At twenty-five paces?" I said contemptuously, for the length of the range scarcely exceeded that distance. "Is it worth the trouble?"

"If you dot the centre of the bull's-eye, my friend," he replied, "it shall stand to your credit."

I chose a pistol, and, taking a careless aim, fired. The bullet struck the white bull's-eye about a quarter of an inch from the centre.

My companion, who had meanwhile likewise made his choice of a weapon, now stepped into my place to take his turn. His aim was quick but careful. I heard the bullet strike the target, but no second dot appeared beside mine in the bull's-eye.

"A pretty clean miss," I said, with a feeling of satisfaction which I could not repress.

He gave me an amused glance.

"Over hasty, as usual, my dear Sir Walter," he said. "Unless you claim to have fired two bullets, I must bike credit for the one that covers yours in the target."

I strode incredulously to the spot in order to investigate the thing with my own eyes. What he said was true. There was but one mark in the target, but, after dislodging the visible bullet with my penknife, I found a second one, my own, buried beneath it.

"By George!" I muttered under my breath; "what a stunning shot!"

"At least, not a likely one for a man who requires to invent lame excuses for poor marksmanship," said Herr von Retzow, who had meanwhile come up behind me.

I said nothing; but, though I could not but acknowledge that the feat I had witnessed was one to command respect, it left me unconvinced on the one point on which it had apparently been his desire to convince me—namely, that his firing at me through the window of the inn at Wittichau had been a mere feint, executed for some purpose best known to himself.

"May I ask," I said, when we had returned to the room we had left a few moments before, "for what object you have summoned me here?"

"To require one more service of you," he replied simply. "It shall be your last."

"You may spare your time and breath, then," I said roughly, "for I shall not be likely to undertake it."

"It would be well, at least," he answered, quite unmoved by my determined manner, "to listen to what I have to propose before you refuse."

He motioned me with a careless gesture to a seat at the further end of the table, and, leaning back in an easy attitude in the chair he occupied, he sat regarding me for a moment with an almost whimsical expression of countenance.

"I may tell you frankly, my dear Sir Walter," he went on, "that it did not enter into my plans that you should learn what you did at Wittichau. But since chance has afforded you an insight into these things, it is perhaps meet that you should have an opportunity of using the knowledge you have acquired. I have, therefore, decided that you shall attend in person the next conference of those of whose secrets you have become possessed."

I hardly knew whether he was mocking me or speaking in earnest.

"Your intentions are extremely kind," I said, with studied irony. "But my interest in the proceedings of these friends of yours is of the slightest, and I have no desire to learn more of them."

"What!" he exclaimed, with feigned astonishment. "Not even for the sake of the Emperor whose cause you champion?"

"Not even for the sake of the Emperor whom you pretend to serve," I replied sternly.

"And can serve no better," he said impressively, "than by the very means I am now proposing. Listen," he went on, falling suddenly into the short, peremptory tone he was sometimes wont to adopt. "The conference I speak of will be held two nights hence, in a room of a certain hotel which I shall name to you. You will attend it unseen, concealed in a closet to which you will gain access from the adjoining chamber. The partition between this closet and the conference chamber is a panel that slides back at the pressure of a button, the position of which will be shown to you by the person to whom you will deliver this letter." He took up a sealed envelope from the table as he spoke. "Neither the panel nor the existence of the closet behind it is discoverable from the other side, but means are provided that will enable you to hear, if not to see, what passes at the conference. Do you follow me?"

"I follow you perfectly," I rejoined, speaking, as before, with ironical politeness; "and pray what is to be the outcome of all this comedy?"

"A pertinent question," he replied. "I will answer it. At a given signal, which will consist in a loud knocking at the door of the room, you will press the button in the closet removing the panel, and pass quickly to the door, which you will unlock, letting in those who demand admittance."

"A likely story, indeed," I said scornfully. "But you will have to select another to assume that part in it which you have assigned to me."

A flush of anger mounted to his brow.

"You refuse to do my bidding?" he asked.

"Your bidding?" I said. "I have yet to learn that there is one who can bid Walter Raleigh do what he would not do. Do you imagine," I added angrily, "that I am to be deceived by so palpable a trap as this?"

"Is that the only difficulty?" he said, pausing an instant, as one who is carefully weighing his words. "You are strangely inconsistent, my dear Sir Walter. Or has it not occurred to you, since you suspect me of these evil designs, that you are at this very moment in a trap from which escape is impossible?"

"How so?" I said, slightly startled, and glancing involuntarily around me; for, truth to say, though I had come here with the full knowledge of the danger I was incurring, the sense of that danger had gradually yielded to the curious influence of tin's man's presence, and I had thought no more of it.

"It is for you to draw your own conclusions," he answered. "But rest assured you shall do my bidding, or abide the consequences of a refusal."

"And what may these consequences be?" I asked in a tone of defiance.

He paused again before he replied, regarding me the while with an air of supreme indifference, which sent a flush of anger to my temples.

"Simply these, my friend," he then said quietly, "that you will leave this house in the custody of the police to answer a charge of murder and high treason."

I sprang to my feet, enraged at the boldness of the thing, and I fear I lost my head.

"Not before I have settled scores with you, double-dyed traitor and would-be assassin!" I cried, hoarse with passion. "If I am to suffer for the crime of murder, I will at least merit my punishment."

I had slipped my hand into my hip pocket as I spoke and whipped out my revolver. But I was too late. Before I could raise and point it, Herr von Retzow, without rising from the table at which he had seated himself when we re-entered the room, had quickly covered me with a similar weapon. At the same moment, apparently in response to some electric signal, the doom in the two side walls opened noiselessly, and a stalwart lacquey appeared on each threshold.

"Disarm that man," Herr von Retzow said in a quiet, even voice. "Nay, if you raise your arm another inch, my friend," he continued, addressing me, "it will be at the cost of your life."

I stood for an instant in doubt. But I saw it was useless to persist. I had to own myself fairly worsted, and I threw down my revolver with as good a grace as I could. Herr von Retzow calmly possessed himself of the weapon, and, having placed it beside his own at his elbow, made a sign to the two servants, who then withdrew again like two automata.

The whole thing had not occupied more than sixty seconds, and certainly, for perfection in its every detail, the incident might have passed for a scene in a well-rehearsed play. In spite of myself, I could not stifle a feeling of respect, nay, even of liking for this man and his strong, dauntless spirit, struggle against it as I might.

He rose from his seat now and advanced towards me until he stood within a couple of feet of me.

"You are stubborn as well as blind," he said, eyeing me sternly. (I could have struck him to the ground, then, and killed him where he stood, for I towered half a head above him, and he had no arms now. Yet I desisted, for what reason I do not know.) "Now, listen to me," he went on. "In your ignorant folly you think it is I who am persecuting you and seeking your life. You are mistaken in this as in many other things, but it is not for me to open your eyes when you refuse the opportunity of self-enlightenment which I have offered you. The mystery that surrounds you has confused your judgment, my dear Sir Walter. Yet there is a clue to it so simple that a child could grasp it. Indeed," he concluded, pointing with startling abruptness to the mantelshelf behind me, where the vial with its ghastly contents, the human forefinger which I had seen him pick up from the snow three months ago, still stood in the same position it had occupied on the night when I first met him, "it is there, within three feet of where you stand."

He noticed the look of perplexity with which I gazed in the direction indicated, and continued—

"Events, it seems, have been crowding in upon you so fast that they have affected your memory, or you would not have forgotten that the man who lacks that finger is still at large. Did I not pledge you my promise that the task of tracking that scoundrel to his lair should fall to you? I am now redeeming my pledge, for you shall meet him face to face two nights hence, and with his capture your troubles will be at an end."

"Do you mean," I said, catching at the bait, though I was loth to believe him, "that I shall find this fellow among those present at the conference?"

"Precisely," he replied. "We begin at last to understand each other."

"But his capture," I said. "There may be half a dozen or more present at this meeting. I cannot deal single-handed with so many."

"My dear Sir Walter," he rejoined, "I would not entrust this man's seizure to even so doughty an arm as yours. Think of nothing but the accomplishment of the task I have set you, which is to throw open the door to those who will demand admittance. The rest will follow."

"It is they, then, who will seize him?"

"Him, and those with him."

"Then why not place them where you would place me?" I objected. "Since access to the chamber where the conference will be held can be gained through the closet, it seems to me unnecessary——"

"My friend," he broke in quietly, "I am not accustomed to argue my plans with such as you. I have given you your choice. Take it. The hour is growing late."

I had already half succumbed to the strange fascination of the man, and if I wavered still, it was rather from the desire to learn more than from any indecision I felt.

"Do you really believe," I asked, "that a promise of services obtained under these circumstances of compulsion is likely to be fulfilled?"

His eye rested upon me with an expression that seemed to search my inmost thoughts.

"Walter Raleigh," he said, with a peculiar emphasis which I cannot describe, "I would not give the value of a silver piece for all the sense you possess. But there are fools who are rich in that most priceless of heaven's gifts—honour, and I believe you to be one of them. I demand your word, no more."

I think I would have struck any other man who had dared to say this to me. All I replied to him was—

"You shall have my word, then, if nothing else will content you. But mark, if you play me false——"

"Enough," he interrupted me with an impatient gesture. "Are you so witless as to suppose that, if I meditated your destruction, I would suffer you to go forth free from here, when with a motion of my finger I could at this very instant forfeit your liberty for ever—nay, perhaps your life itself? Go, my dear Sir Walter, and remember your pledge. Present yourself, the night after next, at nine o'clock precisely at the address on this envelope." He handed me the sealed letter as he spoke. "The poison to whom it is directed will conduct you to the room I have described. Lock the outer door before you enter the closet, and ask no questions; but obey my instructions to the letter. Within three days we shall meet again—for the last time. Good night."

It was his usual form of curt dismissal, and I left him without further demur. There was some truth in what he had said, and I knew it. Yet it seemed to me that there had been a faint tinge of mockery in his reference to our meeting again for the last time, and the memory of it set me a-thinking as I made my way homewards.

During the two days that intervened I scarcely left my lodgings at all, deeming it safest not to expose myself again to the attacks of the murderous villains from whose vengeance I had twice so narrowly escaped. I also took another precaution, which I thought desirable in case of emergency. That is to say, I packed up all my belongings and sent them by the hand of a street porter to the railway station, it being my intention, if I passed safely through the adventure that awaited me, to board the first train that left Berolingen for foreign parts, and betake myself to some country where I should be quit for ever of all the harassing circumstances that surrounded me in the Arminian capital.

Imagine my discomfiture, however, when the worthy porter returned with an air of extreme consternation and placed, instead of the expected luggage receipt, a strip of paper, continuing the following words, in my hands—

"Mr. Walter Raleigh can claim his baggage by presenting this paper at the Central Bureau of the Imperial Detective Police. By Order."

There was no signature to the document, and all the explanation I received from the affrighted porter was, that the paper in question had been handed to him by the official in charge of the baggage room of the station at the Friedrichstrasse, with strict injunctions to deliver it to the owner of the deposited baggage.

I dismissed the man, after handing him his fee, and paced my room in a state of considerable perplexity. Evidently my intentions of flight had been forestalled, a circumstance which filled me rather with impotent anger than with alarm, and caused me to take a step which, to say the truth, I had been too dull, or perhaps too scrupulous, to think of before. It was this. While I had pledged my word to carry out Herr von Retzow's instructions, I had made no promise to refrain from making use of the knowledge he had imparted to me as I thought fit, and I now resolved upon the bold plan of communicating the fact of the meeting of the conspirator's to the Emperor Willibald himself.

My only difficulty was the devising of a means to ensure the safe delivery of my communication into the Emperor's own hands, for I was shrewd enough to conjecture that if it passed, as I knew it must in the ordinary course, through the hands of Colonel von Stauffenberg, it would not be likely ever to reach his Majesty. There was no time to be lost, for it was the morning of the day on which the conference was to take place, and after a hasty deliberation I hit upon the following method. I addressed my warning, in which I stated the precise hour and place of the contemplated meeting, to his Majesty the Emperor Willibald under cover to the general in command of the garrison of Berolingen, and added a short note to the latter, begging his Excellency to deliver the enclosure with his own hands to the Emperor, whose personal safety it concerned.

Having despatched this important document, in which, for reasons of prudence, I gave no clue to my identity, I felt more at ease. All I now had to fear was the possibility that it might reach its destination too late to effect its purpose, for the Emperor, as I saw by the newspapers, was not in Berolingen, but in Potshof, which lies at a distance of about thirty miles from the capital. But I could not influence the course of events. I had done my best and must await the result.

Punctually at nine o'clock that night I presented myself at the address designated, in the letter given me by Herr von Retzow. This was a small hotel in a busy street in the northern part of the town. I delivered my letter at the hotel office, whereupon a personage whom it was not difficult to recognise as the landlord came towards me, and after scrutinising me with a good deal of curiosity, invited me to enter his private room. Thence, without addressing another word to me, he conducted me straightway by a back staircase to the first floor of the building, where we proceeded along a sparely-lighted passage towards what appeared to be a kind of annex recently added to the original structure. He stopped at a door near the end of the passage, and, unlocking it, bade me enter.

I found myself in a small, bare room, littered with rubbish and lumber of every kind, evidently left by carpenters and mechanics who had just finished some piece of work there. A glance around sufficed to show me the nature of this work. A portion of the thick wall dividing the room from the adjoining apartment had been removed, and a kind of closet constructed in the aperture. I was still gazing curiously at this gap in the wall, and wondering at its unfinished appearance, when my companion stepped into the closet and touched a button in the left-hand corner. The back panel slid aside instantly, disclosing a large, well-lighted chamber beyond, furnished with a long table and about twelve chairs. On this side, as I satisfied myself by ocular inspection, the mechanics had put so complete a finish to their work that the most experienced eye could have discovered no trace of their labour. The reverse side of the panel in the closet, as I noted with some amusement, was a life-size painting of his Majesty the Arminian Emperor, of the common, ponderous kind which one usually meets with in the hotels and public places all over the country. The frame was fitted so close to the wall as to give the impression of being let into the masonry, and, indeed, the whole arrangement was so cleverly contrived that I doubt if the most careful inspection would have resulted in a discovery of its real nature.

I returned to the first room, whereupon my taciturn companion closed the panel, showed me once more the mechanism and manipulation of the button, then turned down the light, and left me without uttering a syllable. I heard him lock the door as he went out, and a feeling crept over me similar to what I imagine a rat must experience when it suddenly finds itself imprisoned in a trap.

But I was there, and had to make the best of it. The floor of the closet, which I now proceeded to examine more closely by the meagre light left in the room, was bestrewn with thick carpet rugs, presumably to deaden all sound from my side of the partition. On the other hand, as I stood with my ear close to the panel, I could distinctly hear the occasional creaking of the furniture in the adjoining room. A long and weary wait now followed, and the minutes dragged as if they were hours. Once I heard the door of the next room open and someone move on the other side. But it could only have been some hotel servant, come, possibly, to put the finishing touch to the place prior to the arrival of the guests. At any rate, whoever it was, he passed out again after a while, carefully locking the door behind him, whereupon another long, long pause of silence ensued, to be broken at last by the shuffling of several pairs of feet along the passage.

The door was unlocked once more, and by the whispering that followed I gathered that some, if not all, of the members of the conference had entered the room. Presently the same thing was repeated, and twice more, at intervals of three or four minutes, the newcomers in each case being strictly cross-questioned before they were given admittance.

In all I estimated that about eight or nine persons must be assembled, but it was some time before I could distinguish more than a confused murmur of voices, accompanied every now and then by a peculiar rustling noise, as if papers were passing from hand to hand. Gradually one peremptory voice rose above the rest and thenceforward dominated, seemingly, the whole assembly. I knew the voice well, for it was that of the distinguished stranger whose conversation with the "Doctor" I had overheard in the garden of the hostelry at Wittichau.

I strained my ears now to catch the purport of the proceedings, and though my efforts were not rewarded with complete success, I heard enough to convince me, firstly, that the plot against the Emperor Willibald, of which I had learned the bare details at Wittichau, was far more widespread than I had dared suspect, and, secondly, that it was on the very eve of its consummation.

T wondered, as I listened to the details of this vast political intrigue, the success of which would alter the entire complexion of European affairs, whether it were possible that the Emperor could have realised the full extent of the danger threatening him. Here, within a few feet of me, sat but nine men, but they were the influential leaders of a conspiracy whose ramifications extended throughout the length and breadth of the great Arminian Confederation, and which comprised sovereigns, ministers, diplomats, journalists, physicians, and even two important foreign potentates. Such was the pitch of bitter animosity existing against the impetuous, self-willed young ruler, whose autocratic spirit had more than once come within an ace of setting the world by the ears.

I waited breathlessly to hear some reference by those present to the man who I had every reason to believe had acted throughout as the medium between the parties to the great plot. But, strangely enough, neither the name of Herr von Retzow nor any allusion to him passed the lips of those assembled, though his absence from the meeting should, I thought, have excited some comment. Was the trust these men placed in him so implicit that they harboured no suspicion of the motives which had actuated him in apparently casting in his lot with theirs?

As the time passed, and I listened in vain for the promised signal that would release me from the tension of feeling I was undergoing in the stuffy closet, fresh doubts as to the true object of my presence there began to assail me. What if I were in a trap, after all, and the scheme merely one to expose me at a given moment to the vengeance of the powerful men of whose secrets I had possessed myself? I thought of the taciturn landlord, and remembered, with some misgivings, that he had locked me in the room himself, instead of leaving me to secure the door from within, as arranged with Herr von Retzow. Then, again, I wondered if my despatch had reached the Emperor, and if he would act upon it as I hoped. Whatever might happen, I argued with set teeth, I would at least make my life an expensive purchase, and I instinctively hugged my revolver at the thought.

During these reflections I paid little attention to what was passing in the adjoining room, and it was only when a sudden dead silence fell there that I awoke with a start from my unpleasant reverie. At first I thought that the assembly had dispersed, and that I was left alone, boxed up within these four bare walls. Presently, however, I heard a sound which sent a thrill of excited expectation through me. It was the soft but regular tread of many feet in the passage outside. Had they heard it in the next room, I wondered, and was this the cause of the sudden silence that had fallen upon them? Even as the thought flashed across my mind the sound outside, in the passage, came to an abrupt end, and a moment later two heavy blows were struck upon the door of the adjoining apartment.

My heart leapt within me. The moment for action had come.

"Open, in the Emperor's name!" said a sharp, commanding voice, and during the momentary pause that followed while I searched for the electric button in the closet I fancied that I could hear the deep, nervous breathing of those assembled on the other side of the partition.

It needed but the gentlest pressure, and the heavy panel slid back swiftly, letting a flood of dazzling light into the semi-darkness in which I had been confined. I stepped quickly through the opening, and, looking neither to the right nor the left, passed with two or three bounds to the door, which I unbolted and opened.

I think my sudden apparition must have paralysed the occupants of the room, for no one stirred as I passed through. Now, however, with a movement of actual horror which I shall never forget, everyone present sprang to his feet. In the open door stood, sword in hand, a captain of the Imperial infantry, and behind him two lieutenants, while the passage beyond was occupied by a company of soldiers drawn up in double file.

It was a moment of extreme tension, during which I glanced curiously around at the faces of those assembled. There were in all eleven men present, all standing, with the exception of one who sat at the head of the table on the right hand of the illustrious stranger whom I had first seen in the garden of the inn at Wittichau. As my eye alighted upon this man a feeling of such utter amazement overcame me that I fell back in a helpless kind of fashion upon the very toes of one of the lieutenants who was entering behind me. Almost at the same moment I heard the voice of the captain, who had advanced alone into the room, ring out these words—

"I arrest you, Heinrich von Retzow, in the Emperor's name."

With one frantic movement the person so addressed swept up the pile of papers lying before him and rushed towards the window. But it was too late. Before he reached the window the two lieutenants had seized him and secured the compromising documents.

The captain now turned to the others.

"Gentlemen," he said, "you are my prisoners, and will please answer to your names as I call them."

He drew a list from his pocket and read from it as follows—

"Tribert Leopold, Prince Regent of Wittelsbach."

The illustrious stranger from Wittichau stepped forward with compressed lips and eyes blazing with anger.

"I demand to know," he said haughtily, "by what right or law you dare to commit this outrage upon the person of a federal sovereign?"

"I haven't the slightest idea, sir," the captain answered blandly. "I am a soldier, and my duty is merely to obey my orders. Frederick

Augustus, Grand Duke of Mecklenthal," he continued, reading from the list in a dry, matter-of-fact voice.

The distinguished personage named advanced from the group.

"I join in the protest of his Royal Highness the Prince Regent of Wittelsbach against this gross violation of our sovereign rights," he said.

The captain shrugged his shoulders.

"Charles Frederick of Hohenwerthern, Prince of Brandenburg," he went on unheeding.

The person so addressed stepped forward as the others had done before him. But I heard neither his reply nor the replies of the remaining seven whose names followed. My attention had suddenly become riveted once more upon the man whose presence in that chamber was a source of so much perplexity to me. He was conversing now in a low voice with one of the lieutenants who stood on guard beside him, and from the glances which he every now and then shot in my direction I gathered that I was the subject of his discourse. There was the same look of cold malevolence in his eyes that I had seen in them once before in the room of the inn at Wittichau. But it was not this which exercised so powerful a fascination over me. In his vehemence he had suddenly removed his left hand from between the flaps of his coat, where it had been buried—a peculiar attitude of his which I had often noticed—and as he pointed with it towards the spot where I stood, I observed with an indescribable thrill *that the forefinger of the hand was missing*.

The sight fairly rooted me to the ground, and it was not until I felt a heavy hand laid on my shoulder, and, turning, saw the captain behind me, that I regained my power of speech and action.

"Great God!" I exclaimed, addressing that officer and pointing towards Herr von Retzow, "who is that man?"

"One in whose company it is dangerous to be caught, as you see, my friend," he replied simply. "Vorwarts, we have no time to dawdle."

He gripped me roughly by the arm and I fell back thunderstruck.

"What!" I exclaimed, freeing my arm with a quick wrench. "Am I to understand that you arrest me, too? On what grounds? I am innocent of any complicity in this vile conspiracy. The Emperor knows it, and none better than he."

But my expostulations fell upon deaf ears. In a twinkling half-a-dozen soldiers were around me, and I was overpowered and made a prisoner like the rest.

What it all meant I was utterly at a loss to conceive. For an instant, as I glanced instinctively across at Herr von Retzow, who stood between his guards eyeing me with a look of villainous triumph, the horrible suspicion flashed across me that, after all, my warning had not reached the Emperor, and that my seizure as an accomplice of the men whose treasonable schemes I had been instrumental in thwarting was but a prearranged part of the deeply laid plans of the astute police agent himself. And yet, if this were so, how could I account for the fact that he, too, had been taken prisoner? Was his arrest merely an act in the farce in which I had so foolishly assisted? or was it the result of extraordinary miscalculation on his part?

The captain now gave the word of command, and the soldiers falling into double line, with their prisoners in their midst, the curious procession filed out of the room in military order. To all appearances every other occupant of the place had taken flight, in the street, also, every vestige of the busy traffic I had encountered there on my arrival that night had disappeared. But drawn up in front of the hotel stood a row of some dozen carriages, with a soldier seated motionless on the box of each. Into the three first of these the captain and his two lieutenants entered with the three princely personages whose names I had heard called, and the three conveyances were whirled rapidly away—to what destination I knew not. The rest of us followed into the remaining carriages, and were driven away in an opposite direction. Within ten minutes the conveyance I was in drove through a dark archway and drew up before the door of a large square building. I alighted and was conducted up a short flight of steps into a capacious office, which I recognised at a glance as a police bureau. Here the formality of my transfer from the military to the civil authorities was effected, and I found myself entered upon the records of the station as "One Walter Raleigh, foreigner. Political suspect."

As I was being led away to the cells I made one more endeavour to remonstrate against the treatment I was receiving. But the police official paid as little heed to my energetic protests as the captain had done before him. I was left in the darkness and solitude of my narrow police cell to ruminate upon the extraordinary events of the last few hours and the probable fate that awaited me.

THE INCIDENT OF THE MAGIC CARD AND THE STORY OF AN IMPERIAL DETECTIVE

I DID not close my eyes that night. Since the commencement of the strange series of adventures which I have been relating, nothing had so completely confounded me as this last, to me, most puzzling experience. I had been prepared for treachery on the part of Herr von Retzow; I had even conceived the possibility that in plotting the betrayal of his fellow-conspirators he had boldly schemed to rid himself of me at the same stroke; but his own presence at the meeting, which he must have known was destined to end so dramatically, was a mystery that baffled me utterly.

Had it been a part of his whole treacherous plan, and was his own arrest merely a blind to safeguard him against the vengeance of those he was betraying? The more I revolved the question the more obvious the answer to it seemed. But, think as I might, I could find no plausible explanation of the startling fact that the man with the missing forefinger, the desperado to whose murderous onslaught I had nearly fallen a victim when I sprang to the assistance of the stranger in the Thiergarten four months before, was apparently none other than Herr von Retzow himself.

That I should have unwittingly gone home with the very man who had sought my life, thinking that it was he whom I had befriended, was a mistake almost too absurd to appear possible. Moreover, what could have been his object in suddenly patronising the very individual upon whom a few moments before he had been so eager to wreak summary vengeance?

I recalled all the incidents of that fateful night from which my recent strange adventures dated. All I could remember was that I had been stunned by a blow while wrestling with my assailants, and had lain—for how long I knew not—unconscious in the snow. When I recovered my senses I had found no one beside me save the man whom

I had since known as Herr von Retzow, and I could have sworn that he was the person to whose defence I had sprung.

Could the forefinger in the snow, which I had seen him pick up and afterwards preserve in so ghastly a fashion, have been his own? I tried to recollect, but in vain, whether I had ever seen Herr von Retzow's left hand. I had noticed the peculiar trick he had of burying one hand between the flaps of his coat, but the habit had never aroused my suspicions. And, indeed, how could it? Even now, with the evidence of my own eyes before me, the supposition that I had all these months associated with my deadly enemy was so monstrous that my understanding revolted against it.

While I was struggling to reconcile all these strange contradictions, the thought of my own immediate fate almost faded from my mind, and it was not until long after daybreak that I began to consider all the possible consequences of my present awkward situation. From what I had learned of the system of secret trial and punishment of political offenders in Arminia, I knew enough to convince me that my position was one of extreme danger. If, then, my conclusions were correct, and Herr von Retzow had purposely contrived to have me present with the conspirators at the moment of their seizure in order to compromise me in the eyes of the authorities, there was little doubt that he would bring forth such false testimony at my trial as would suffice to convict me of participation in the very scheme I had really been the means of thwarting.

I groaned aloud at the thought of my utter helplessness to clear myself of such a charge. There was but one person who knew of my innocence, the Emperor, whom I had myself warned of the plot that was threatening him. But even if I succeeded in procuring the testimony of so august a witness, was it not more than likely that I should thereby expose myself to a new danger? I had crossed swords with a member of the Imperial family and had killed an innocent girl—the latter by accident, no doubt, but under circumstances which would scarcely palliate my crime in the eyes of the iron-minded young autocrat, whose jealous notions of the divine prerogatives of royalty no one had yet been known to offend against with impunity.

In short, the longer I dwelt upon all the puzzling aspects of my case, the more desperate it appeared to grow; and when, at last, towards the noon hour—as I supposed, for my watch and all other effects upon my person had been taken from me the night before—my cell door was unlocked, and I was told that I was to appear before the judge to undergo the preliminary examination, which is in Arminia the equivalent of our proceedings in the magistrate's court, I followed my guards with a feeling of reckless indifference born of despair.

The room to which I was now conducted was not an ordinary court room, but a chamber of comparatively small dimensions, furnished with a long table covered with green baize, behind which sat three clean-shaven personages, with a formidable array of papers piled up in front of them. There were a few common wooden chairs placed in a row against the wall facing these men, on one of which I was ordered to seat myself, whilst my two conductors sat down beside me. Otherwise the room was bare of all furniture, and, with the exception of a dried-up old clerk, who passed backwards and forwards between this and the adjoining chamber, carrying bundles of papers and documents, there was no one present but the three judicial individuals behind the table and I and my two guards.

As soon as I had seated myself, the middle personage behind the table raised his head and regarded me for about thirty seconds with a cold, scrutinising glance. Then he ordered me to stand up, and proceeded to question me rapidly as follows:—

"Your name is Walter Raleigh?"

I replied in the affirmative.

"You are a foreigner?"

"I am of English birth," I said.

"You arrived in this city four months ago, on the 25th of last January?"

"I do not remember the exact date," I replied, "but I presume it is correct."

"For what purpose did you come here?"

"To seek employment," I answered.

"What kind of employment?"

"I am a soldier by profession," I said; "I hoped to enter the service of the Emperor."

"And failing in this purpose, you entered the service of his enemies?"

"If I did so," I said earnestly, "I did it unwittingly and with no evil intent. His Majesty himself can testify to my loyal intentions towards his person."

The judge waved his hand to check my speech.

"Silence," he said sternly. "You are here to be questioned, not to offer suggestions."

"I am here to defend myself," I said boldly.

"We shall see," he answered. "Let the indictment be read to the prisoner."

The reading of the document which now followed occupied about ten minutes. It was a tissue of barefaced lies from beginning to end, and under ordinary circumstances I should have found no difficulty in refuting every one of the charges contained in it. But, hemmed in as I was by dangers and difficulties on all sides, I had no means of defence save a flat denial of every count in the indictment.

Needless to say, my chief accuser, upon whose evidence the case against me mainly rested, was, as I had anticipated, Herr von Retzow himself, and, judging by the cruel ingenuity of his statement, and the completeness of detail which characterised it, I could only conclude that it must have been prepared for some time. To my surprise it contained no allusion to my presence at the hotel the previous night, nor did it make any mention of my supposed complicity in the plot against the Emperor Willibald. I was accused of being the leading spirit among a gang of foreign anarchists, whose aim was the assassination of the heads of the reigning dynasties in Arminia; and in support of this accusation numerous compromising letters and documents were cited, all of which purported to have been discovered and seized in my lodgings by the henchmen of Herr von Retzow.

I had no doubt that these papers were impudent forgeries, concocted for the express purpose of ruining me. But how was I to prove it? My capture the night before, in the very midst of a bevy of Arminian sovereigns, afforded seemingly the strongest confirmation of my guilt. Even my brief term of office as Oberstallmeister to the Duchess of Bieberstein was construed as evidence of my sinister designs. The position, it was declared, had been procured by fraudulent documents, and my assertion that it had been Herr von Retzow himself who had placed me there was received with derision. I demanded in vain to be confronted with this man. I was told that at the proper time and place I would be brought face to face with the witnesses in the case, and hear from their own lips the evidence they adduced against me.

"It would be better for you, however, young man," the judge added, eyeing me coldly, "if you made a free confession of your guilt, and divulged the names of your vile accomplices. We have means of extorting these which better men than you have been unable to resist."

"I cannot betray accomplices who do not exist," I replied. "But I am ready to tell my story, if I may do so in my own way and without interruption. Perhaps," I added, "it may throw some light on matters of greater import than the guilt or innocence of the humble individual who stands before you."

"Proceed," said the judge; and I entered into a detailed description of my adventures since that fatal night on which my acquaintance with Herr von Retzow commenced, laying particular stress upon my discovery of the conspiracy against the person of the Emperor, and the detailed knowledge I had obtained of its ramifications and the names of those concerned in it.

The three persons behind the table listened with immovable countenances, only now and then exchanging some remark in a whisper, or taking written notes of what I said.

When I had concluded, the middle one of the three spoke again.

"Your story is a very foolish one," he said, "for it is manifestly impossible, and bristles with palpable lies. Do not imagine," he continued, with a touch of anger, "that you can succeed in confusing the minds of your judges on the subject of your own guiltiness by the introduction of matters pertaining to the crimes of others. The knowledge you pretend to have obtained regarding these things will avail you little, for it is less complete than that which is already in the possession of the authorities. The examination is over. Remove the prisoner."

The last words were addressed to the constables in charge of me, and my heart sank within me as they fell upon my car. I heard the judge direct an order to be made out for my solitary confinement in the prison of Moab—a place associated in my memory with many a grim story of political persecution; then a sharp tap on my shoulder from one of my gaolers signified to me that I was to withdraw. The prospect of weeks, perhaps months, of solitary imprisonment, with little chance before me of ultimately regaining my freedom, made my blood run cold, and with a violent effort I shook off my two custodians, who had now gripped me each by an arm.

"Stay!" I cried; "you will surely permit me to produce proof of the truth of what I have said. I have such proof, or, rather," I corrected myself, "you have it, for my pockets have been rifled of their contents."

"To what do you refer?" the judge said.

"Give me my pocket-book and my papers," I replied, "and l will prove to you that this man who accuses me of crimes I have never committed was himself my patron and self-constituted protector. I have it in his own writing."

I spoke excitedly, for the thought of the card given me by Herr von Retzow, which once before had stood me in such good stead, had suddenly flashed across my mind. I felt but little hope that it would do so again under these altered circumstances; but it would at least, I thought, go some way towards proving my veracity.

The judge hesitated an instant, then touched a bell, and ordered the clerk to bring in the articles taken from my person. The pocket-book was handed to me, and I turned over its contents with nervous hands. But all my fumbling was of no avail. The card was nowhere to be found.

I stammered some incoherent excuse, and begged that the other effects taken from me should he searched through.

"I swear," I exclaimed, "that the card was in my possession last night."

"We are wasting time," the judge said, with an impatient gesture.

"Gentlemen," I cried in desperation, "as I hope for salvation, I repeat that it was in my possession last night. If you would not let the most dangerous of his Majesty's enemies escape the punishment he richly deserves, you will leave no stone unturned to discover the card."

"It is enough," the judge said, after searching the papers. "Here is no card. Let this farce end."

He waved his hand to the constables, and the sweat stood out on my brow. As a last resource, more in despair than from any hope of finding the precious piece of writing, which would perhaps not only disclose the true nature of my relations with Herr von Retzow, but also implicate Colonel von Stauffenberg, the Emperor's secretary, in the treasonable designs I still attributed to him, I plunged my hand into my breast-pocket, where I had always kept the card. To my intense satisfaction I found it there, caught probably in the lining of the pocket, where it must have escaped the attention of those who searched me.

With a gesture of triumph I held it aloft, and at a sign from the judge one of the constables took it from me and handed it to him.

I can hardly say what immediate effect I had expected from its perusal by those upon whose decision my present fate turned. That it would delay my removal to the prison of Moab, and perhaps cause me to be confronted at once with my villainous accuser, was certainly what I hoped for. I may even have been sanguine of better results still, such as a greater inclination on the part of my judges to give ear to, if not exactly to credit, my protestations of innocence. But in my most wildly imaginative mood I could never have conceived the possibility that this crumpled slip of paper would produce the effect it actually did upon the men who a moment ago had sat there stern and inflexible, recking but little whether they condemned an innocent man to a long term of slow and torturous suspense, or not.

I can still see the middle one of the three deliberately adjust his glasses the better to examine the paper, and then, after casting a cursory glance at its contents, start up with every sign of excessive surprise and consternation, and pass it on to his two coadjutors, who in their turn exhibited the same signs of confusion at sight of it. Had a bolt from the blue fallen suddenly into their midst, it could scarcely have created a greater sensation.

"How did this paper come into your hands?" the judge asked me at last, regarding me with a look of undisguised interest.

I repeated the story I had already told, saying that the card had been given me by Herr von Retzow with injunctions not to use it except in a case of dire extremity.

"It was this man," I added, "who, for purposes of his own, procured me the office of Stallmeister to the Duchess of Bieberstein, and at whose instance I was present at the meeting of the conspirators last night. What part Colonel von Stauffenberg played in his nefarious doings is beyond my knowledge. But if you value the Emperor's safety it will not long be beyond yours."

There was a hurried consultation between the gentlemen behind the table, the purport of which I was of course unable to gather. Then he who had questioned me before spoke again.

"This matter shall have our immediate consideration," he said; "let the prisoner be removed to the cells."

Before I could reply, all three rose hastily and retired from the room, whilst I was led back to my cell and left there to ruminate alone on the strange scene I had just witnessed.

Once before, as I well remembered, I had seen a similar effect produced by this seemingly insignificant piece of writing. It was on the night of my adventure in the house on the Waldstrasse. The recollection was like that of some dream-like vision, blurred and indistinct, but still definite enough for comparison with what I had just now experienced. Was it a mere coincidence? Was Herr von Retzow still in possession of his old power? Had I mistaken his intentions, after all? And if so, how could I explain this cruel and libellous indictment, and, worse than all, the bewildering fact that he himself was the man with the missing forefinger?

These, and innumerable other puzzling questions, tortured my brain as I paced my cell waiting for some ray of light that would pierce the darkness around me. At last, after two hours of suspense, my cell door was once more unlocked, and a lieutenant of police stood on the threshold. Notifying me curtly that I was to follow him, he conducted me, not back to the court room, as I had expected, but through a series of passages to a back outlet of the building leading to the courtyard. Here stood a droschky, which he bade me enter, and, having given the driver some direction in a low voice, he jumped in after me, and we drove away at a rapid pace.

Was I to be confronted with my accuser? I wondered. Or was I on my way to the prison of Moab? I glanced once or twice inquiringly at my companion, who sat beside me cold and taciturn; but I knew the genus too well to suppose that it would be of any use to question him as to our destination, and, not feeling in the humour to brook an insolent answer tamely, I contented myself with noting the direction taken by the vehicle and speculating on its ultimate goal.

So far as I could make out, we were driving due east; and for a time I imagined, with a sense of growing satisfaction, that I was on my way to the house of Herr von Retzow, near the Thiergarten. But just before we reached the Avenue of Limes, which is the dividing line between the eastern and western portions of the city, we turned sharply to the left in the opposite direction, and sped up the quiet street that leads in the rear of the Imperial palace to the Place of the Opera. Here we drew up suddenly at the entrance of a big, almost windowless, building, and the officer motioned to me to descend.

"You had better pull yourself together, my friend," he said, not unkindly, as I alighted and looked up with a sinking heart at the bare wall fronting the street. It had an ominous resemblance to a prison. "You are to have an audience with the Emperor, and will want all the wits you possess."

Before I could realise the meaning of it all I was inside the building, which was apparently a rear portion of the Imperial residence, and a few minutes later found myself in a big square chamber occupied by a number of military big-wigs, who eyed me and my conductor with looks of supercilious contempt. The worthy police officer, as I noted, was scarcely less ill at ease than I myself, and, having brought me so far, appeared now at a loss what to do next. Presently, however, an adjutant approached us, and, after exchanging a few whispered words with the lieutenant, disappeared through a curtained door to the right. In a few moments he reappeared, and dismissing my companion, signed to me to pass through the curtained entrance.

I obeyed almost mechanically, for, truth to say, my wits were totally scattered, and I felt as timid and helpless as a frightened child. I heard the swishing sound of the big double door as it swung back into position after I had entered, and looking up, knew at a glance that I was in the Imperial cabinet.

At a huge table near the window, littered with countless papers, stood the Emperor. He was perusing a lengthy document, which bore a strong resemblance to the copy of the indictment I had seen the judge read from a few hours ago, and it was some time before he deigned to notice my presence.

Then, after scanning me for a moment from the distance with a slight frown on his brow, he beckoned to me to approach.

"You are the late Stallmeister to the Duchess of Bieberstein, I understand?" he said, addressing me in his strong guttural Arminian.

I replied in the affirmative, taking care to speak in the same tongue.

"Your adventures in my capital appear to have been of a somewhat varied character," he continued.

"I can assure your Majesty," I said, "that they were not of my own seeking."

"Pshaw!" he answered, with a touch of impatience, "that is a child's excuse. You are charged with being the ringleader of a gang of anarchists. What have you to say in your defence?"

"That the charge is preposterously false!" I cried determinedly. "If your Majesty will but permit me to be brought face to face with the dastardly villain who has concocted it——"

"Let that rest," the Emperor broke in sternly. "The day of retribution has already overtaken this man Von Retzow, and he will suffer for his crimes as he deserves. As for you, it would be well if you looked elsewhere for evidence to clear yourself of the grave suspicions that rest upon you."

"If you will deign to listen to my story, sire," I said, with difficulty repressing an exclamation of delight on hearing that the arch traitor Von Retzow had, after all, met with his deserts, "it will at least prove that I have been innocent of any evil intentions towards your Majesty."

"Maybe, sir," he said, shooting one of his piercing glances at me, "I already know more of your story than you bargain for. My police have watchful eyes, and it would be strange if you had escaped them. But proceed," he concluded curtly, "and be brief."

Thus admonished, I plunged once more into a hurried account of my life in Berolingen, from the memorable night of my encounter with the three ruffians and the stranger in the Thiergarten until my arrest the night before, and my simultaneous discovery that the man with the missing forefinger was none other than Herr von Retzow himself. There was only one incident which, for obvious reasons, I passed over in silence—that of my duel with the Duke of Friedrichsburg and its tragical issue on the evening of the Imperial masked ball.

The Emperor listened with a grim expression on his countenance, which never altered. Once or twice he threw in a quick, impatient question, but otherwise gave no sign that the recital of my strange experiences aroused more than ordinary interest in him.

When I came to the story of my adventure in the hostelry Zum Alten Fritz at Wittichau, not thinking in my eager haste that I had already recounted its main features to him on the occasion of the masked ball at the palace, he interposed with a gesture to prevent me from repeating it, and I faltered on, in some confusion, to an account of the events that followed my escape from the inn, the attempts made upon my life in the streets of Berolingen, and my last interview with Herr von Retzow, with its strange and, to me, unaccountable consequences.

When I had concluded, his Majesty fixed me with a penetrating look.

"Save for certain omissions, which mar its completeness," he remarked coldly, "your story is entertaining enough. But perhaps those incidents of your career which you have thought fit to conceal are in your opinion of too trifling a nature to be remembered."

"I have told your Majesty everything," I stammered, with a sense of guilty fear, "which bears upon my present unfortunate position."

"On the contrary, sir," he answered, "you have told me everything which does not bear upon what you are pleased to call your present unfortunate position. Or are you foolish enough to suppose that an attempt to assassinate a member of the Imperial house, and the ruthless slaughter of an innocent woman, are crimes that go unpunished in this country?"

I believe he expected to see me stand covered with confusion at this sudden revelation of his knowledge of the events in the palace garden. But I had anticipated it and had steeled myself accordingly.

"Sire," I said earnestly, "if the sacrifice of my own life could restore that of the unhappy lady who died, as your Majesty must know, by my hand, but not by my will, I would make it willingly. As for my encounter with his Highness the Duke of Friedrichsburg, it was a fair and honourable combat, as the Duke himself will testify, and one for which I offer no excuse, unless it be," I added boldly, "for having dared to teach his Highness a lesson in fencing which cannot but have proved to his advantage."

I expected to see his Majesty fly into a passion at this last cut, and, truth to say, I cared at that moment naught if he did. But nothing of the kind occurred. Whether the humour of the thing tickled him, or whether he liked the boldness of my speech, it is certain that he received it without show of anger.

He turned away with a brusque movement, and strode across the room. Then, returning again, he confronted me at a distance of a few paces.

"It is well for you," he said, "that his Highness the Duke has generously pleaded for you, or the lesson, as you call it, would have cost the giver more clearly than hint who received it. Nay," he continued, advancing a step nearer to me, as if to give greater emphasis to his words, "but for the fact that you have rendered me some service in aiding to bring this wretched villain Von Retzow to justice, you should still suffer the full penalty of your crime."

I made a movement expressive of gratitude for this unexpected show of clemency, but he checked me with a frown.

"You owe no thanks to me," he said. "It is upon the intercession of one whom you have scarcely served as loyally as he had a right to expect that the Emperor deals thus leniently with you. He owes you a debt. I have repaid it."

He paused an instant, as if he awaited some reply, and then continued in a slow, deliberate tone—

"It appears that you have succeeded in making for yourself the reputation of being a good swordsman, but a very sorry diplomat. *And, in truth, from what I know of you, my dear Sir Walter, I would rather entrust my safety to your sword than to your wit.*"

The last words, which were spoken in the purest English—a language I had never heard from the Emperor's lips—fell upon my ear like a thunderclap. The tone, the accent, the very voice itself, so different from the stern, abrupt voice of the Arminian Emperor, staggered me as if I had suddenly received a message from the grave. I had heard these identical words once before, only, as I thought, from very different lips, and certainly in very different surroundings. Gradually, as I stood staring at the man before me as if he were a ghost, every feature in his face grew strangely familiar to me. Only the boldly upturned moustaches left me an instant in doubt whether it could be possible that he was one and the same with the Herr von Retzow I had known and associated with all these months.

But the doubt was dispelled at once. As he stood there, with his left arm partly concealed beneath his military coat, in the characteristic attitude the remembrance of which had puzzled me so much these last twenty-four hours, I understood for the first time why I had never seen the supposed Herr von Retzow's left hand. For does not all the world know that his Arminian Majesty's one arm is partially crippled from birth, and that it is always carefully hidden from the sight of men?

There is a certain class of puzzle the solution of which is at first sight even more bewildering than the puzzle itself. The mystery which had surrounded me so long was revealed at last as in a flash, but the revelation almost surpassed in its strangeness the mystery itself, and left me floundering in a sea of seemingly irreconcilable facts. One thing alone stood out at that moment with painful clearness in my mind—that the Emperor, who had already astonished the world by playing pretty well every *rôle* known in human society, from judge to parson, had now deigned to act the part of his own detective, and had done it, as he did everything, with a tolerable measure of success. The hot blood rushed to my head as I thought with shame of the incredible blunders I had been guilty of. What a grand opportunity I had blindly wasted! To have associated all this time unknowingly on terms of practical intimacy with the Arminian Emperor himself, and this to be the outcome of it all. The thought was maddening.

The Emperor stood regarding me for a considerable while in silence, evidently enjoying ray discomfiture. Then he took a soiled and crumpled slip of paper from his table and tore it into fragments. It was the card I had handed to the judge a few hours before.

"Now that your eyes are opened," he said at last, resuming his usual curt and decisive manner of speaking, "you will comprehend what has impelled me to adopt so lenient a course with you. Let the suspense you have endured serve as a warning to you to respect in the future the sanctity of those whom Heaven has placed as far above you as the stars are above the earth. If you go hence a free man, it is upon the condition that you leave Arminia within four-and-twenty hours. Mark that. If you overstep this time of grace by the space of but one hour, nothing shall save you from suffering the full penalty of the law."

He dismissed me with a wave of his hand, and I went without a word. I had a thousand questions upon my lips which I would have gladly asked him had I only dared. But the difference between the genial and fascinating individual with whom I had passed so many pleasant hours and the stern and imperious personage I was now confronting was too overwhelming and cowed me completely.

I returned to the humble quarters I had left nearly four-and-twenty hours ago with my mind in a state of complete revolution I was free again, it is true, and the world stood open to me once more much in the same way that it had stood open to me four months before. And yet, curiously enough, now that my adventures in Berolingen were at an end, and nothing was left for me to do but shake the dust from my feet and betake myself to some other quarter of the globe, I felt a strong reluctance to quit the scene of so many strange and thrilling experiences. Such, I suppose, is the changeable nature of human desires. A few hours before, I would have purchased my escape from that very scene with almost any sacrifice that might have been demanded of me. Now, the thought of my forced departure filled me with a feeling of fiery resentment.

Perhaps, had I then recalled to my mind certain incidents that had passed between me and the man whom I had all along believed to be the famous police agent, I must have admitted to myself that they were not exactly calculated to ingratiate me with his self-opinionated Majesty. But, after all, was I to blame for the many errors I had committed? Even now, as I sat ruminating over the details of my life during these few months, it was only very gradually that the whole solution of the complicated mystery dawned upon me, and I realised how strangely I had been deceived. It was clear to me, of course, that the stranger to whose defence I had sprung that night in the Thiergarten was the Emperor Willibald, and that the attack upon him, which I had so opportunely foiled, was committed by the real Herr von Retzow, probably for the purpose of finding out the identity of the person who was penetrating his dangerous secrets by appearing disguised as the famous agent himself.

Had not the night been so dark, and other circumstances so disadvantageous, I should have seen the face of my principal assailant, and possibly solved that part of the riddle from the start. All my subsequent mistakes originated there. Hence I could not guess that the face I saw some weeks afterwards at the window of the house in the Waldstrasse was that of the real Von Retzow, who, having schemed in vain to possess himself of the marriage certificate of the Duke of Friedrichsburg, had contrived to induce the Princess of Bieberstein to proceed in person to Wittichau in order to convince herself of the fact of the Duke's marriage. That he was the man who intercepted her Highness during her memorable ride in the Thiergarten and placed the mysterious slip of paper in her hands was fairly certain. For had I not noticed that the forefinger of the fellow's left hand was missing, and even reported the fact to the Emperor himself? It was doubtless he, too, who had received the packet of papers that evening at the house in the Waldstrasse, and from whom they had been forcibly recovered again by the Duke of Friedrichsburg.

What infamous blackmailing design had been at the bottom of all this curious business I could only guess at. Possibly it was connected with some secret Court intrigue, and Herr von Retzow had been merely the paid instrument of those concerned in it. Only one thing was certain—that the Emperor had discovered his agent's plans and had employed me to foil them. I could not but marvel at the skill with which this Imperial detective must have tracked his man step for step and brought his nefarious doings to light. And I, after all, had been but a mere tool in his hands, and a somewhat troublesome tool at that. I understood now the full extent of the blunder I had committed at Wittichau. Here again, needless to say, it was the real Herr von Retzow whom I had met and so recklessly threatened, nor could I doubt that the murderous attacks which were subsequently made upon my life in the streets of Berolingen had been instigated by him.

How extraordinarily simple it all seemed, now the one solitary clue to the riddle had been revealed to me. Clearly, his Majesty had never contemplated such a thing as my discovery of the conspiracy against his person, nor, perhaps, had he any reason to be grateful to me for the part I had taken in exposing it. He had merely intended to utilise me as a kind of spy upon the Princess of Bieberstein and her surroundings, probably regarding the question of the Duke of Friedrichsburg's betrothal to that sweet Princess purely as a side issue between himself and his opponents.

And here was a point which, in the light of this conviction, remained for some time a source of much perplexity to me. For what purpose had the Emperor insisted upon my presence in the closet during the meeting of the conspirators? It is true he had enjoined me to note carefully what was said and done by those assembled, and I had certainly heard enough on that occasion to convict half the notables at the Imperial Court, and a few crowned heads besides, of complicity in the plot to depose his Arminian Majesty. But then, if I had really been employed as an eavesdropper that night, why was I never called upon to adduce the damning evidence I had gathered?

To those who are familiar with the details of the remarkable trial that followed the arrest of Herr von Retzow the answer may be obvious. But it must be remembered that many months elapsed before the particulars of that trial reached the public knowledge, and I learned that the documentary evidence seized that night at the hotel was far more complete than any testimony I could have given, a fact which doubtless rendered my appearance at the trial unnecessary. In short, the Emperor had laid his plans only too skilfully, and had not only caught all the ringleaders in the plot at one fell stroke, but had captured the written proofs of their treasonable purposes at the same time.

All the world knows now what an infamous career of crime was brought to a close by the arrest of the man whose very name had become a terror to Arminian society, even including some of the highest in the land. But what hand the young Emperor himself had in bringing this villain Von Retzow to justice, and at the same time foiling one of the most gigantic political conspiracies known to history, has never been disclosed. There was but one single man arraigned before the tribunal whose proceedings excited the attention of all Europe for the space of many weeks, and although the number of those, far higher in rank and station than he, whom his trial compromised, was such as to completely dumbfound the public mind, there are, even to this day, hut few initiated persons who know the true history of their connection with his criminal career, and perhaps fewer still who have any conception of the imminent danger in which his Arminian Majesty stood in those days.

Does not ancient history tell us of some great leader of armies who ended by having altars erected to himself? There has always been something vastly tragical to my mind in this pathetic record of history—the collapse of self-achieved greatness. Whether history will repeat itself in the case of the present Arminian Emperor—who can say? If it does, it will require on the latter's part something more than the mere building of altars to render the comparison quite perfect.

But I have run ahead of my story, or rather of its conclusion, for I have but little left to say. In story books that I have read, adventures far inferior to mine, though possibly better told, have conducted men to fame and fortune. My harvest was disgrace and banishment. Not that I cared much for the disgrace, which I felt to be undeserved, nor perhaps had I any reason to grumble at being banished from a country where my experiences had been so bitter and unpleasant. Indeed, though I left it unwillingly, I did so with but one regret—that I was not permitted to see the fair Princess again who had once been my mistress. Since those days she has become Duchess of Friedrichsburg and sister-in-law to the Arminian Emperor. But I have never ceased to think of her as the sweet, winsome girl she then appeared to me, pure and innocent, untrammelled by the restraints of her illustrious station, spirited, natural, and impetuous—to my notion the very ideal of sweet girlhood.

To be quite frank, it was the sense of failure that rendered my departure from Berolingen so bitter, for I had undoubtedly failed, let the cause have been what it may: and so I went, with my pride humbled and ray hopes crushed. I was saved the humiliation of having to claim my baggage from the police, for it was brought to my lodgings within an hour of my return from my audience with the Emperor.

With it came a packet of bulky appearance, stamped with the seal of his Majesty's privy chancery, which on opening I found to contain five hundred pounds in Bank of England notes. Accompanying this not unhandsome gift was a short note, which I may transcribe here as the most fitting conclusion to my strange narrative. It bore a signature that had become only too familiar to me, and ran thus—

> "Depart in peace, my dear Sir Walter, and remember that a hot head and a foolish tongue are apt to anise more mischief than a good sword can cure. Keep silent on what von have seen and heard, and you shall not regret it.
>
> "H. v. R."

I leave the reader to judge whether the last passage of this note does not convey a tacit promise of reward to come. If it does, all I can say is that this promise, during the years that I have maintained silence on the subject of my extraordinary adventures, has remained unredeemed. I need offer no excuse, therefore, for the publication of the facts I have now related; for, indeed, when kings and princes forget, why should ordinary folks remember?